To
Josephine
from Grandma.

The Children "Going Through."

PALMER COX,

Brownies AND OTHER Stories

ILLUSTRATED

BY PALMER COX.

THE STORIES TOLD IN PROSE
By E. VEALE,
The Fairy Tales Authoress.

NEW YORK
HURST & COMPANY
PUBLISHERS

The Brownies' Visitors.

THE Isle of Fun and Frolic was the home of the Brownie boys and girls, and no one can e'er deny that the island was well named. These youngsters had no thought but to run and play, to sleep and to eat. They loved the flowers and they loved the birds—and the butterflies led them lively chases in their games of hide and seek. But one day came a change in their lives, and they learned that others lived in the world besides themselves. Little Peak Hat discovered it, as she stood on the rock looking out toward the sea. It was a great vessel ploughing the waves, its white sails flapping in the winds, and as she watched she saw it moving steadily toward the island. All the Brownies came rushing at her call, and their wonder knew no limit. On came the vessel, closer and closer; the Brownies watched as long as they dared, and then, fearful of being seen, hurried away to hide themselves where they might occasionally take a peep. What great big creatures were landing on the island, and what loud voices they had as they called to each other. It sounded to the Brownies like the roar of distant thunder. All day long

5

the little people remained hidden, but when night came they stole from their hiding places to talk it over. What kind little hearts these Brownies had. All the nice pieces of wood should be

piled up for these strange people's comfort, the best grapes should be saved for them, they would coax the fish to nibble, and do all in their power to make these queer guests happy. Indeed they

seemed to think of nothing else, and had you
visited their home in the old forest, you would
have found them busily engaged in planning
how they could add to the comfort of their
strange guests. The Brownies are never so happy
as when they are busy making others happy.
They believe that the best way to enjoy life, is
to give pleasure to those they meet. Of course

 the visitors did not
know what was mak-
ing their visit so
pleasant, for these
busy little creatures
always work quietly
and secretly. The vis-
itors did not stay
long, but the Brown-
ies did good service,
and when they had
gone, they quite
missed the pleasure they had felt in making others happy, and they were continually
wishing that some favoring wind would bear
some other ship to their shores that they might
again have an opportunity of renewing their
acquaintance with these queer people,

The Fairy Queen's Palace.

ALL the Brownies had promised to help, and when a Brownie undertakes a thing he works as busily as a beaver until it is accomplished. Now this is what they determined to do.

The Fairy Queen's palace had been destroyed — a w i n d that had swept through t h e forest carrying trees before it, and spreading ruin as it traveled, had lifted up the Fairy Queen's home and dashed it all to pieces. Poor little Queen; how sorrowful she felt to lose the pretty house where the royal family of Fairyland had so long lived.

8

But true to their nature the Brownies came to
the rescue, promising to build a palace far more
beautiful than the one that was lost. Such help-
ful little creatures as the Brownies never lived.
No chance of doing good to one in trouble ever
escapes these generous little fellows, and certainly this was a work to be hailed with much joy.

For a long while before they commenced, you
could see them gathered in groups, discussing
how and where they should begin, and how they
could make the palace more beautiful. They
were a funny looking set when they started out
for the place where the house was to be built.
Each one carried something. One little fellow
had an axe; another, hammer and nails, one the
mortar hod, and still another the plane, while
the master worker could be seen with the square
in his hand giving directions to the whole
crowd.

They commenced their work one beautiful
moonlight night. Brownies, you know, work
when the darkness has put all the world to sleep.
What a time they had getting all the things together. Arriving at the spot, some fell to chop-
ping wood, while others mixed the mortar and
rigged up the pulleys by which they were to raise

the stuff to the roof. How the hammers rang out as they struck the bright little nails. The grindstone went spinning around so fast it hummed quite a tune, as the carpenter sharpened his tools, for the Brownies had so much to do they must work their very fastest. The plasterer mixed the mortar; the painters made their brushes fly over the house; the masons worked with a will at the chimney, and the paperhanger's scissors shut with a click as he cut off the paper for the palace walls, which were to be so prettily decorated.

When morning came, all was finished, and the Brownies felt proud and happy as they looked at their night's work. They worked as if by magic, and almost before you could think, the palace rose high in the air. The Brownies don't have accidents very often, but they must have been nervous this time, for while four or five of them were seated on a "Jack" painting the outside, over went the paint, brushes and all, and the little fellows who were standing on a ladder underneath had an unexpected bath.

They were only sorry to think that they had left their camera at home, for they would have been happy to give the children a picture of the house as it looked when it was finished.

Although they were tired, and their eyes were growing heavy with sleep, they felt repaid for

all their efforts, especially when the Fairy Queen seemed the proudest and happiest of them all. She thanked them heartily for their loving service, and when they had seen her safely settled in her new home, they all disappeared, to be seen no more until there was more good work to be done.

The Brownies' Plum Pudding.

'TWAS the evening of the twenty-fourth of December. The clouds had been gray and heavy all day, and now the snow flakes were beginning to fall thick and fast, so fast that already quite a white blanket was spread over the earth.

This did not please the Brownies; they had work to do, and a snow storm would hinder rather than help its progress.

Somewhere in the woods, nobody knew where, for the Brownies kept the secret all to themselves, was a great big Christmas Pudding full of plums and citrons, raisins and spices, and the Brownies wanted to bring that pudding home.

It was so big and heavy that they had built something that made one think of a raft or perhaps a ladder with the sides very far apart. How they put the pudding on it would be hard to tell, but they managed it and bravely they struggled with their burden perched on their little shoulders. They took turns so that no one got too tired, but all were glad when they were safely out of the woods and had landed the pudding in the hollow of the old tree back of the school house, for this had been the spot chosen for the grand feast of the morrow. Then to their homes they skipped away to dream of the good times in store for them, and if their backs did ache and their poor little feet felt sore and weary, the vision of the pudding dancing in their heads made them forget all their woes.

And what a treat they had on Christmas Day! The pudding was so good, and the day was so merry that the Brownies wished, as they shut their sleepy eyes, that Christmas came more

than once a year. They made up their minds
that they would never let a Christmas go by

without having a plum pudding, for it was the
best thing they had ever tasted.

The Raid of the Insects.

SHE was Queen of the garden, this beautiful
creature, and all the flowers loved her. Each
vied with the other in trying to please her. The
tall white lilies held their heads still higher as
she passed by, the tiny bud opened its curled
petals further and further until it burst into a

glorious rose, the blue bells tinkled their sweetest music, and the shy, gentle mignonette shed

forth its loveliest perfume—every flower did all
in its power for her sake.

And the Queen loved all the flowers, too. She begged the sun to shine down upon them, and she asked the morning dews to bathe their bright faces, and the gentle rains to give them plenty to drink.

At last there came a day when the lilies hung their heads; blue bell and heart ease fell from their stems; the poppies that had gleamed so

brightly in the sunlight covered their faces and shone no more, and all the garden seemed full of gloom and sadness.

The insects had done it all. With their sharpest weapons they had attacked the flowers, making them one by one yield to their violence.

How this grieved the Flower Queen; but at last she thought of the Brownies, and she smiled,

for well she knew these clever little workers.
She found a trumpet flower that had escaped the

cruel foe, and blew one gentle blast. Quick as
a wink the Brownies came running. Their faces

looked sad when they heard the trouble, but
they promised to do all in their power to help
their gentle Queen, and bravely they went to
work. They took turns at the grindstone and
sharpened their spears and swords and axes until
they glistened in the moonlight, and the insects
might well have trembled had they seen
them.

In the morning when the sun peeped out to
waken the flowers, the insects once more started
on their raid, but they were not prepared for
what followed. Curled up underneath flowers
and bushes hid the Brownies. Out they rushed,
and war raged fiercely; but the Brownies came
off the victors, and the bees and the beetles, the
hornets, ants and caterpillars lay dead upon the
ground.

The Brownies' Wedding Gift.

ONCE upon a time, long, long years ago, there
lived somewhere the other side of the Atlantic
Ocean, a maiden who was as beautiful as an
angel, and better than being beautiful, she was
also good and gentle.

Elsie and her father lived alone, for her mother had died many years before, and this beautiful maid kept her father's house, and managed all things like some wise and noble queen. The poor people of the village loved her, for it was her gentle hands that brought broths and strengthening food to the sick mothers, her beautiful eyes that read comforting words to the old women, and in her untiring arms many a poor little baby had been rocked to the land of dreams.

There was somebody in the village who loved her better than all the people put together, but he dared not tell her, for he was poor, very poor, and she was rich as a young princess. Now it happened that the maiden loved the youth as much as he loved her, but she was too proud to show her love, because she thought that the young man did not care for her.

One day great changes came to the home of Elsie. Her father had gone on a journey, and when he returned he did not come alone but brought with him a wife, and she brought with her two proud and unlovely daughters.

It was a great trial for the maiden; she and her father had always been so happy

together, and she wept when she thought of how little of his time and love could now be spared for her. Well might she weep—for the new mother set right to work to put her daughters in the place of Elsie, and with cruel words and taunts compelled her to wait upon these step-sisters, until her life became one dreadful burden. Tales, unkind and untrue, were carried to the father, and when his wrath was turned upon her she could stand it no longer, and made up her mind to leave her home forever.

One night, when they all had gone to a ball,

to which Elsie also had been invited, but from which she had been compelled to stay away because her beauty so far out-shone the gaudy make-up of the sisters—she packed a few treasures, and with many tears and farewell glances, for the spot she loved so well, she went alone into the great, wide world.

It chanced that Earnest, the youth who loved the maiden with all his heart, had grown restless and unhappy thinking of his sweetheart, and yet not daring to tell her his love, and he had come to her home thinking that perhaps he might find comfort in being thus near her. He wandered up and down, when all at once he stopped, looked around him, and then rubbed his eyes—for he surely must have been dreaming; this could not be Elsie who stood before him. But it was she and no other—poor Elsie leaving her home, sad and broken-hearted.

Pride no longer held the youth speechless, and sorrow made Elsie see the tenderness and sympathy in her lover's eyes. Oh, how happy she was as she poured out to him all her troubles and found comfort and rest in his loving arms.

While the lovers stood together planning a life for the future—things had been entirely taken out of their hands by the good little Brownies.

They had known Elsie, and worshipped her for her goodness, and now the time had come when they might show their appreciation; and while the lovers talked, they had gathered silently around them. Then the Queen of the Brownies spoke: "Good and lovely maiden, and noble youth," said she, "we know of your troubles, and we want to help you. Listen to what I tell you, and you shall have riches in abundance. Go, when I have finished talking, enter the Briarly woods. There, in the hollow tree, you will find a casket filled with bright and shining gold; take it, spend it wisely, and take with it the blessings and good will of the Brownies." It was a wonderful wedding present, and filled the lovers' hearts with gratitude.

The Brownies and the Farmer.

THE Brownies were sorrowful, more sorrowful than they had ever been in their lives before, and that is saying a great deal; for Brownies, you know, live such a long, long while, and the saddest part of all was that there seemed no way out of their trouble. The Brownies who lived in the apple orchard saw it first, and when they told their friends, all with one voice cried out: "The wrong must be righted!"

Now this was the trouble. Farmer Grump had bought the Old Clover Farm, where the Brownies had lived happily for years, and now each day was full of trials and discomforts, for this cruel farmer seemed always to be finding a way to make the life of his stock miserable. The cows had great boards tied over their eyes—so large that they could not see, and so heavy that when the poor creatures went to crop the grass, Bang! Bang! went the board against their noses.

The pigs suffered, too, Into their noses had been driven rings that almost made them bleed when rooting in the ground. And what happiness do you suppose life holds for a pig if he cannot root?

The Brownies liked the donkey, for he seemed such a patient, long suffering animal; but the farmer's children made his life wretched—they beat him, they stoned him, they even took their naughty little feet and kicked him.

The sheep suffered, and the horses, as they dragged the plough through the hard earth or hauled heavy loads along the sandy roads, felt constantly the slash, slash of the farmer's cow-hide whip.

Everything on the place suffered; so, do you wonder the Brownies looked sorrowful?

At last they could stand it no longer, and all met one night at the "Seek us further" tree,

where the oldest Brownie lived. He had gotten up in the limbs, so that all might hear, or, at any rate, see him, and announced that they had long witnessed these scenes of cruelty in silence, but now something must be done, and they wanted all the Brownies to help. He thought it

would be a good plan if they went when no one
was around, and whispered in the sufferers' ears
that the time had come when they must rebel.
They must stand up for their rights.

"Hurrah!" and "Three cheers!" cried the
Brownies in chorus, as they waved their funny
little hats. The farmer heard the noise, but he
thought it was only the wind blowing through
the trees in the apple orchard.

The meeting was dismissed, and quietly and
carefully the Brownies went about their work—
and they did it well, too; for the next morning,
when the farmer went to harness his horses, and,
as usual, brought the cruel whip down on their
back—he found that two could play at the same
game, for up went the horses' heels, and sorry
trouble Farmer Grump had to get them har-
nessed.

Then the pigs took their turn. They showed
their long white tusks, and acted so savagely
that the farmer left them in fright. Even Ned,
the patient donkey, kicked up his heels, gal-
loped away, and no one could come near him.
Everything seemed possessed with the same
spirit, and Farmer Grump went to his breakfast
the most puzzled man you could possibly find,

But the animals won the day, for that very afternoon the farmer went to town, and when he
came back he was carrying a large board painted
in great big letters, telling all the neighbors that
his stock was to be sold the very next day. This
he hung up by the roadside, and as it was market
day, the farmers learned the news, as their tired

horses jogged slowly along towards home. They
decided that they would attend the sale, and
were on hand bright and early the next day.
The old farm place was crowded with buyers,
anxious to get horses and pigs and other animals
for little money.

How happy the Brownies were as they
crowded around, for the new owners had thrown

the cruel devices of Farmer Grump away. They were happy when they thought of the good homes these poor animals had found—but gladdest of all were they when they thought of Ned, for Widow Love had bought him to cart to market the beautiful butter that she made every week. They knew that she would be very kind and gentle to their old friend. That he would have the softest of straw for his bed at night, and the finest oats for his dinner, while there would be no cruel children to beat and kick him and make his life miserable. Ned lived a long while to enjoy this beautiful home, and the Brownies always found him a faithful servant.

The Brownies' Ride.

"ARE you in the humor for a lark, boys?" It was Dot, the very smallest, and, as everybody knows, the most mischievous of all the Brownies, who said it.

"We are that!" was the reply.

They were coming home from school, these Brownie boys, and dinner pails and books were

thrown down at once while they crowded around
Dot to hear of the prospective fun.

"You know that clover field to the right of

the big stone house," he began. "Well, some
time ago Grimes put up a sign, which read:
'Horses taken to Pasture.' You should see the
luck he has had. I guess as many as a dozen

horses are running around in that pasture field. It's bad for them to do nothing but eat all day, so I thought we would be doing a good thing for them, and for ourselves too, if to-night—you know it is moon-light—we borrow these horses and go for a ride."

You should have heard the yells of delight with which this scheme was greeted. Nobody but approved, except, of course, Croak; he always objects to everything.

The plan was for them to meet at the school-house at ten o'clock, then go together to the pasture lot. A number of the Brownies were to bring ropes, which they would tie around the horses' necks, and haul them into the road.

The hour came; the Brownies met, and the work began. They had forgotten saddles, but some of them crawled through the windows in the harness maker's shop and came back loaded with both saddles and bridles. Such a time as they had getting them on, and so many Brownies had been invited that there were not enough horses to go around; so two, and sometimes three saddles must be put on one horse.

All was ready at last, and off they started. It was so funny to see them. Some of them actually

hung on to the stirrup straps. Things went
pretty smoothly at first, but, oh my! what a
difference by and by. Saddles slipped, bridles
came undone, and the Brownie boys, and even
the poor horses, went over and rolled around in
the mud. But the bitter must be taken with the
sweet, so nobody dared complain. When the
ride was over, and the horses and harness were
put in their proper places, everybody pronounced
it one of the best frolics he had ever had in his
life.

The Quarrel.

THEY were rivals—the Gobbler and the
Gander. Their home was at the Brookside
Farm, and it would be hard to find a prettier
home than this. It was a big old-fashioned
house, and it had stood for years and years. The
brook ran along on one side, and day after day it
babbled as it flowed, and the little daisies lifted
up their pretty heads to listen to its merry
songs, and when night came their drowsy heads
dropped as the brook murmured a low, sweet
lullaby.

The gander had been enjoying the cool, clear waters of the brook. He had thought himself a very beautiful bird, as he sailed gracefully up and down, arching his long white neck with a perfect air of contentment. The other geese at the farm were quite young, some of them so young that they looked like little lumps of yellow gold as they plunged boldly into the water. And why should they fear? For the brook had murmured, coaxingly: "Come, little baby bird. Come bathe in my waters; I will not hurt you; I will sing you low, pretty songs." The gander remembered when the brook had gently called to him, and he smiled as he thought how long ago.

His swim over, he had come on shore, and once more donned his cap and trousers, and even better satisfied than ever, had started home for his dinner.

"Ha! Ha! Ha!" he heard behind him, and again, "Ha! Ha! Ha!" Turning around, whom should he see but the gobbler rigged in his very best, his tail spread out just as wide as he could get it, and looking very grand indeed, even the gander had to admit as much as his eyes rested upon him,

"Don't you think you are a sight!" said the Gobbler. "Go look at yourself in the brook over

yonder; you'll surely agree with me that a more ridiculous bird than yourself never lived."

"Ridiculous, indeed!" replied the angry Gander. "If you but knew what a sight you were, never again would you strut around the barn yard!"

"Strut do you call it?" exclaimed the Gobbler. "I pride myself that my walk is most elegant. Now, if I waddled as you do I'd hang my head with shame."

"'Tis but your jealousy that makes you talk so," said the Gander; "you think because you are tall and your legs are long, that you'll be much admired and praised—but people do not notice you when I am sailing on the waters; then it is that you must stand in the background, and my short legs and broad-web feet serve me as your feet and legs never can you."

Word followed word, and these foolish birds grew angrier all the time. The rooster stopped the quarrel, for their loud words had attracted the other birds. "Do you know," said he, "you have kept up this foolish nonsense so long that now you have lost your dinner? 'Tis an hour ago since Ann came with her shining tin pan full of corn, but you paid no attention to her. To-day's loss is a small loss, but it might have been much greater. Do hereafter remember

your positions, and try to act more like grown-up
fowls, than like two tiny, newly-hatched birds.
Remember that the little folks of the barnyard
look to you as an example."

The Dissatisfied Owl.

BLINKY WINKY was a little gray owl that lived
in the plum tree at the meeting of the cross-
roads. He slept all day, and at night perched on
one of the branches and greeted the wagons as
they went by with a low "Whoo! Whoo!" He
did not mean to be inquisitive, only pleasant and
friendly, at least that is what he used to do, but
now he has grown very quiet and solemn, and
heeds not the wagons as they go rumbling by.

The lark had been the cause of all the trouble.
In the early spring she had come to live across
the road from Blinky, and her song, so sweet
and clear, filled his whole heart with wonder
and awe. "If the lark can sing," thought
Blinky, "why can't I?" And he tried to throw
back his head and pour forth the same sweet
tones, but this was impossible with his short fat
neck, and his mightiest effort was of no avail

So day by day Blinky grew sadder and sadder, but still the lark sang on, not knowing what unhappiness she brought to poor silly Winky.

One night he left his home, more miserable than ever, and perched himself upon the fence rail to brood over his troubles. It was a bright moonlight night, and the owl family that lived in the apple tree saw Blinky Winky sitting all alone, and started off, one after the other, to bring him home with them. Such a doleful bird as they found. It was a long while before Blinky would tell them his secret, but once started, he poured forth his whole sad tale. They pitied and they scolded him, and their scolding did him good, for when morning dawned, and it was time to go home, they had led him to see the folly of his ways and to resolve to try to be satisfied with himself, and not aim to be like somebody else. He learned, after spending many unhappy days and weary nights, that God had not made his little throat in such a manner that he could sing. It was a good lesson for him and all his brothers and sisters. Perhaps little boys and girls can learn something from this story of the dissatisfied owl, and it is this: "Don't think you can do everything you see other people doing."

Meddlesome Peter.

THE Bear family lived together in as pretty a place as you could well find. The trees grew tall and large and spread their branches over the earth, leaving only room enough for the sun to creep gently through by day, and for the little stars to twinkle brightly through at night. Ferns tall and stately grew in this place, and delicate, pale green ferns with the gentle blue-eyed violet peeping from their midst, helped to beautify the Bear family's dwelling place.

The Bruin household would have been just as happy as Bears could be, if it had not been for troublesome Peter. He was the oldest Bruin cub and just as full of naughtiness as was possible, and his greatest fault was his meddlesome ways. There was nothing into which he would not poke his paws.

One day, while out on a ramble, he spied a bright, shining steel trap. Now Peter had never seen one before, and quick as a flash he grabbled it up to learn all about it, and he soon found out to his sorrow. Snap went the spring, and poor Peter howled with pain. Fate was good to Peter this time, for as he jumped around in his

fury, the spring gave away, and off came the
trap, leaving young Bruin, however, with as sore
a paw as ever you could guess.

Now, one would think that this experience
would prove a good lesson to Peter; but no
sooner had his paw gotten well than he had forgotten all about his encounter with the trap and
was at mischief again. Mother Bruin coaxed,
Father Bruin scolded. Peter always tried to do
better, but his memory usually proved too short,
and promises went for nothing. One bright
spring day he started off through the woods to
hunt for fun, as he called these foolish pranks
with which he was constantly dealing. He
chased the butterflies, hurled stones at the hop-
toads, and then sat down on the ground to eat
the wild cherries that had fallen from the thickly
laden boughs. Now Peter's eyes were always
wandering restlessly around, and all of a sudden
they rested on a big hollow in a tree close by.
"That's a squirrel's house," thought Peter. "I
wonder if the little fellow has any nuts left over
from last winter; I'll go see, I guess." With
Peter to think was to act, and he thrust his paw
away down deep in the hollow. Peter had found
something, but not nuts. The bees had discov-

ered this place first and were using it as their

store-house for honey. Now Peter's intrusion
was not to their liking, and their sharp little

stings soon told him so. They swarmed all
around him, until he felt as if he were covered
with them, and the faster he ran, the more they
chased him. He could neither run away, nor
hide from them. Not until he was well punished
did they leave him, tingling with pain, but resolved, we hope, to once more try to do better,
and not to meddle.

Poor, Sick Bruin.

ONCE upon a time, when Jack Frost had commenced to shake the leaves from the trees after
first painting them in bright crimson and glow-
ing yellow, and some in dull russet brown, Mr.
Bruin fell sick. He had been to a dance in the
Kingston Woods. Miss Bunny had invited him,
and old Bruin had thought her the brightest,
cunningest little creature he had met for many
a long day. Of course she was too tiny for him
to dance with, but he sat and chatted with her,
which he really thought was much pleasanter,
at least he had thought so at the time, but now
he was paying for his frolic. The ground had

been too damp and cold, and the chill winds had
gotten into his bones, and he was the most miserable fellow you could possibly find.   "O dear,"

thought he, "why was I so silly.   Well might I
have known what folly it was to leave my good
warm home, and spend all those hours out in the

chill night air." But it was too late to sit and
grumble over follies that have been committed,
so Bruin wrapped himself in a green plaid shawl,
tied up his head in a red and white handkerchief,
and sat to wait for Dr. Wolf to pass along. Dr.
Wolf had been called to pay a visit to a little
sick guinea-pig, and his way led him past old
Bruin's house. Bruin saw him, called to him,
and the doctor came trotting in. He took off
his tall black hat, laid it on the table, put on
his glasses, and prepared to examine his patient.
The doctor felt his pulse, shook his head, and
then looked at his tongue. "Oh, ho! my friend,"
said he, "you have caught a cold, that is certain;
but, my good fellow, I am afraid there is something more. I fear that you feast too much upon
the dainties of the land. Your larder seems well
filled with tempting food, but if you take my
advice you will leave this alone for awhile, and
content yourself with a good big bowl of mush
and milk. You have a very high fever, and if
you eat of such rich food you will surely die. I
am going to put you to bed, and you must not
get up for a week; you are getting along in
years, so you must take extra care of yourself.
I shall leave you some pills to take every hour,

unless you are asleep. I shall be passing here again in the morning, and will drop in to see you. I hope to find you much better." Then the doctor went away, leaving Bruin a sadder and wiser bear and resolved in the future to try to live more simply, and to let his poorer neighbors share the dainties that had proved his foe.

The Squirrel's Visitor.

In the Maple Woods, just outside the town, lived an old gray squirrel. He was a big squirrel and just as fat as butter. One time, long ago, he had been caught in a rat-trap, and his leg pretty badly torn. A bright-eyed, red-cheeked boy had found him, and carefully and gently had lifted the heavy wire frame, and had taken Frisk out. The poor little squirrel was hurt and frightened, and the boy felt sorry for him. He carried him home in his arms, and then wrapped him in a soft, warm blanket and put him in a basket. He meant to doctor his wounded leg and keep him for a pet. Frisk, however, did not like this notion, and in the morning, when the

boy came to find his prize, the basket was empty
and Frisk had hopped away on three legs.

Frisk was so frightened that he never got over
it. He lived in a hollow tree all by himself, and
each night when he put his night-cap on, he

slipped his pistol under his pillow. One night,
when the wind blew furiously and the rain came
dashing against the tree, Frisk sat all alone,
thinking how good it was to have such a nice,
warm house and so many delicious nuts stored
away, when, tap! tap! tap! came against the side

of the house. Frisk was frightened, but he grabbled his pistol and peeped cautiously out of the door. Not a sign of any one could he see, so he went quietly back. Tap! tap! tap! came again. Once more Frisk looked out, and there stood a poor, drenched wood-pecker. He had been out hunting worms for his wife's supper while she stayed home upon the eggs. He had been overtaken by the storm, and now sought shelter with Frisky. How they laughed when Frisky showed him his pistol and told him how frightened he was, and that he had thought him a burglar.

Frisky insisted on his friend's coming in, and resting with him in his comfortable, snug little house until the storm was over. Then he filled his friend's basket with the choisest bits his store-house afforded, and sent him away happy.

The Wolf's First Party.

THE wolf had been invited to a party, and his head was almost turned by this piece of good fortune, as he thought it. The fox had sent him the invitation, written in big round letters

on a piece of birch bark. "Miss Fox requests
the presence of Mr. Wolf at a party in the hollow," the invitation read, and the wolf felt as
though he had some standing in the world now,

for never before had any one called him Mr.
Wolf.

He got up bright and early the morning of
the eventful day, and hurried from among the

leaf-covered trees to hunt for the sun that was just showing her smiling face above the hill, behind which she had hidden all through the night. The wolf gave her a friendly nod, and gazed at the blue sky with feelings of the greatest pleasure. He felt he could scarcely bear it if the rain should fall, for he had almost reached the limit of his patience in waiting for the party, and the rain would mean that he must wait still longer. But on this bright spring morning there were certainly no signs of rain. Early in the afternoon the wolf began getting ready. He washed his face and hands in the little brook that splashed and sang as it danced over the stones, and then, as it grew broader, flowed gently and silently along. The brook was the wolf's mirror, too, and a pine cone served him for a comb. The poor, silly wolf was ready hours before it was time to start, and he wondered if one always felt so anxious over their entrance into society. He wondered, too, if he were really not more nervous than little Miss Fox.

But at last the time of departure arrived, and the wolf started off. He must have something to carry, for he did not know what to do with his hands; so, remembering that some one had told him that you had better have an umbrella and not want it, than to want it and not have it, he carried his big green sun-shade.

He was the first to arrive, and Miss Fox was so pleasant and made him so welcome that he never felt so happy before. Nor did this happiness end, for when all the guests had taken leave, the wolf remained to tell Miss Fox that this had been the best and brightest time in all his life. For many days he thought about the fine times he had had at his first party, and wondered if he would always have such fun, and if all the ladies were as nice as Miss Fox.

The Crow.

DID you ever notice a number of black objects flying through the air or perhaps assembled in a flock hunting for worms, or caterpillars, or grubs, or maybe feasting on some fallen grains? These are crows, and if you could examine them closely you would see how beautifully their glossy, black wings are tinged with dull blue and brown and purple. They are very shy and cunning and very fearful of the farmer's gun, with which they seem to be well acquainted. One of them serves as watchman, and when he sees danger approaching he sounds the alarm, and all the crows within hearing distance fly up and away. The eggs of the crow are laid in nests made of sticks woven with grasses and lined with soft roots, feathers, or wool. Both the father and mother bird sit on the eggs, and watch with great care over their young. The crow can fly very swiftly, and sometimes to great heights, and it can also fly long distances. Have you ever noticed one perched on a cow or perhaps a sheep's back? It has perched itself there to pick the worm out from the skin. Their cry of Caw! Caw! Caw! is very ugly, and what a din they make when they gather together in little parties early in the morning to go in search of food, or else at night when they are hunting for some pleasant roosting place. The crow is a very brave bird and is not afraid to attack the hawk that sometimes comes swooping down upon it. Its sharp, black eyes are of great service in its search for food—indeed it is upon this sense that it depends and not upon the sense of smell. Its keen sight also protects it from the attack of the

enemy. Sometimes you come across a crow that
is perfectly white, but this is not the case often.
The crow makes a very amusing and interesting
pet, except that it has the bad habit of stealing.
Thousands of crows are killed every year by
traps or the farmer's gun, and often and often
the poor little young ones are killed in their
nests by the hands of cruel and naughty boys.
The crow does steal the farmer's grain and pull
up the young seedlings, but he would be less
merciless to the poor bird, if he only saw how
much good he does in destroying the worms and
bugs, the mice and moles, which really eat up
lots and lots more than the much abused black
crow. Sometimes the farmers set up "scare-
crows" in the fields to frighten the thieves away,
but they soon learn that it is only a make-believe
man, and are not afraid.

Bruin's Visit.

JACK FROST was raging around in all his fury;
great white flakes fell thick and fast and settled
one above the other upon the ground, making a
blanket soft and warm for the little plants that

lay hidden under the earth. The trees moaned
and shook their boughs as the wind went whistling through them, and the little snow birds
hopped gracefully from limb to limb hoping to
find a stray worm or bug to satisfy their hungry
little selves.

Bruin had started bright and early that morning to visit his cousin, a brown bear who lived in
the woods beyond the school house. It was a
long journey, but Bruin cared little for that, for
he knew the way, and knew also the good times
that he and Cousin Bear enjoyed together. Well
he remembered his last visit. What sport they
had playing ten pins, with sticks for pins and
stones for balls. How they enjoyed the game
of catch with the big horse chestnuts that fell
from their prickly coverings and lay scattered on
the ground. The snow had put a stop to ten
pins and catch, but it had brought sport of its
own, for what better fun could two young bears
want than a jolly game of snow-ball or a ride on
the school-house hill? With all these good times
dancing in his head, Bruin started off. Mother
Nature had given him a thick furry coat, but
old Jack Frost did his best to pierce through this
heavy brown covering, and make him hurry

along to keep good and warm. The school house came in sight as he turned the last corner, and Cousin Bear's home was soon reached.

How glad Cousin Bear was to see him. They chatted away as busy as beavers, for there was so much to tell and so much to hear, but all was told at last, and then arose the question—what next to do. Snow-balling was fun for awhile, but their paws got too cold. They could not go up on the hill, for all the school children were out with their sleds, and there certainly was not room for them both.

"Let's have a game of hide and seek," said Cousin Bear.

Bruin liked that idea and cheerfully consented. Cousin Bear shut his eyes, and Bruin hurried off to find some good hiding place. First he tried one and then another, but nothing suited him, until at last the very thing met his gaze. Time had worn a great hole in an old oak tree. There it stood, bending its leafless limbs as though beckoning Bruin to crawl inside. Such a splendid chance could not be missed. My! how good and warm it was. Bruin was tired, and before he knew it he had gone sound asleep. How long he slept he did not know, but when he opened his eyes the shadows had crept heavily over the woods, and night was coming on apace.

Cousin Bear started in surprise when Bruin rushed breathlessly into his house, for as he could not find him he thought he had gone home, and then how he laughed when Bruin told of his hiding place, and they both thought it a great joke that Bruin had fallen asleep, while he was playing. He said he would remember to look there for him next time they had a game.

Bruin warmed himself by the bright fire, and then said he must be going. Cousin Bear would not hear a word as to his leaving until they had had supper. So he set out the very best his storehouse afforded, and they both had a very merry time, eating the turkey and fat little lamb, which the bear had stolen the night before. When they had cleared the table and washed the dishes, Bruin trotted off towards his home as fast as he could. It was dark before he reached his own woods, but he was not afraid, for he knew every step of the way. He was pretty well tired out when he got home, and it did not take him very long to get ready for bed. As he curled himself up for a good long sleep, he felt satisfied over a very happy day.

The Owl and the Bat.

"Good evening, Miss Bat," said the grave gray owl, "pray may I come up and chat awhile?"

"Indeed, you may, Mr. Owl," replied the bat. "It's such a beautiful evening that I have been sitting up here ever so long watching the moon, as she played hide and seek among the trees; the stars seem to be enjoying the game as much as I, for they twinkle as brightly as diamonds so far above us all."

"I see you have an eye for the beautiful, my dear young lady," said the owl, "but if you but knew it, the most beautiful thing I have seen in all my life is yourself."

The bat hung her head and looked quite shy, while the owl blinked his eyes and looked as though he thought he had really said something most elegant.

you know, my dear," continued the owl, "I have watched

you night after night as you floated around so
gracefully, never interfering with the other birds,
but going quietly about your own business, and
I decided that some day or other I would ask you
if you would not consent to be Mrs. Owl. The
time has come, Batty dear, and I hope you will
say yes."

The bat did say yes, for she had long admired
the owl. She liked his solemn ways, and thought
him a very handsome bird.

It was decided that they should be married
very soon—the very next week, in fact, for the
moon would be shining in all her glory then, and
the guests could not be asked to come in the

dark, even though it might be pleasanter for the bride and groom.

The stork wrote the invitations. He wrote them on the leaves of the water-lilies, using his long sharp beak for a pen.

The night of the wedding came, and with it many guests. The stork and the crane came together, for they lived in the same pond. The eagle and the buzzard met as they came sailing through the air.

The happy pair were soon made one, and then what merry times they had. The lark and the nightingale sang their brightest songs, and all joined hands in a lively dance. Morning came only too soon, and the guests must go, and as the owl kissed his little bride, he wished that all her life might be just as happy as the first night had been. What a happy time the bridal party had for the next few weeks. When the guests had all gone, they packed their trunks, and hastened away to spend their honey-moon among the pine forests of the Green Mountains. They traveled from place to place, journeying by night and resting by day; for strange as it may seem, these queer creatures can neither of them see when the beautiful sun is shining.

Thy have such curious eyes that the light makes them blind. So they used to spend the long summer days nestled close together on the branch of some high tree. At night they would fly about here and there, watching the other animals and enjoying the pure air.

The owl is a very wise bird, you know, so he was able to tell his trusting little wife many interesting things.

After spending a very pleasant time, they returned to their home, and settled down to spend a very happy life.

Unhappy Bruin.

Poor Bruin's life seemed marked with misfortunes. Bruin was not one of the happy creatures who have the good fortune to be born under a lucky star—the night must have been cloudy and most miserably starless when he opened his eyes in this wide, wide world. As the years went on poor Bruin's troubles seemed to grow. Fortune had no kindly smile for him, and try as he might, all his efforts to succeed were in vain.

One time Bruin left his home, and went strolling through the woods. He was all alone, for the other bears had gone off long before, but Bruin had not been wanted. Sorrowfully and lonely he trotted along, taking no heed of where he was going, until all at once he was brought to his senses by a sharp click, and try with all his might, he could not move. You've guessed what had happened—he had stumbled into a trap, and was held there as fast as fast could be. The hot sun poured down upon him, but no one came to release him; but at last, just as twilight fell upon the world, two great big men drove up in a cart, and with a loud shout at their horses, stopped

in front of Bruin. "Fine luck we have had to-
day," said one of them. "We will make a good
thing out of him," said the other. Then, as
quick as a wink, a big black bag was thrown

over Bruin's head, and he was hoisted into the
wagon.

This was the beginning of poor Bruin's new
life. These men were street players—one of
them brought forth squeaky sounds from an old

fiddle, while the other made most dismal noises
upon the harp.

Bruin was taken to their miserable home, and
day by day was trained to dance and play tricks
to amuse the people. Bruin found it was wisest
to please these men, for cruel blows and kicks
rewarded his failures.

One day they rigged him up in a suit of
clothes, put shoes on his feet and a hat in his
hand, and led him out to dance upon the street.
All day long he kept it up, and when night came
he could scarcely move. His masters had gone
to join some friends and chat with them, and
had left Bruin in charge of a boy. The boy
grew tired of being alone, and seeing a chum,
hurried after him, leaving Bruin to his own devices. Bruin knew his chance had come, and
trotted away just as fast as ever his tired feet
would carry him. He wandered on and on, until
at last the woods were reached. Then he lay
down under a tree, nearly worn out, but very
happy he felt that at last the wheel had turned
and fortune had surely smiled on him.

The Ostrich.

DID you ever think anything about the way in which we obtain the beautiful feathers that help to ornament our hats and bonnets? Away off, in a country called Africa, lives a bird known as the ostrich. It is a large bird with long, slender legs, and such a great long neck that it is as tall as a very tall man. Nature has given it these long legs to help it go over ground very rapidly. When pursued, it travels across the sandy plains where it lives with strides that carry it twenty-five miles an hour. The ostrich has very keen sight and sharp hearing, and its long neck aids it in seeing great distances.

The nest where the mother bird lays the eggs is just a hollow made in the sand, with a shallow border all around it. The old bird sits on the eggs and keeps them warm at night, but the rays of the hot tropical sun do the work in the day-time. These eggs are very large, weighing from two to three pounds.

The baby ostriches are very pretty birds. They look like young partridges, only they are many, many times larger and have little bristles all over them mixed with down.

When the ostrich is about a year and a half
old it falls a vistim to the hunter's pursuit.
There are a number of ways for catching them.

Sometimes the hunter clothes himself in the
skin of the bird, and imitates its motion so exactly that it is almost impossible to tell the sham

from the real bird. Then, when he is within bow-shot of some unlucky bird, his arrow pierces it, and it falls his prey. Sometimes the bird is caught with a lasso, and in some places the hunter mounts on horse-back and pursues it in that way.

Way off in California there are a number of ostrich farms, and when you get to be big, perhaps you will be able to go there and see them. But the very next time you go to the Zoological Garden, you must get your mammas to take you to see these wonderful birds. I am sure you will wonder how such beautiful feathers can come from such ugly looking birds.

King Leo's Resolve.

MOTHER NATURE had carpeted the earth with a covering soft and brown and rustling. Deep in the reds and yellows she had dipped her paint brush, and the trees gleamed in their grandeur like a flaming forge. The squirrels had been busy for weeks filling their store-houses with the nuts that would serve for the winter's food, and the song of the birds had long since ceased, for far away they'd flown, seeking a warmer home. All the woods seemed hushed and forsaken.

King Leo noticed all this as he paced through the forest with restless strides this autumn day. Things had gone wrong with his majesty, and he wondered that the trees should glow in such brilliancy when all else seemed dressed in sombre colors. "Why must nature," muttered he, "have this dash of brightness in her adorning while my life is all gloom and all sadness? Long have I reigned in the forest as King of Beasts. I've held sway over the largest of them all, the tigers, wolves and bears have trembled at my roar, and at my command all have yielded. Now I'm deserted. No longer am I consulted in affairs of wisdom. It's months since I have sat on my throne of holly boughs. I'm forsaken and alone. Is there no way in which I can win them again? Must all my life be thus, sorrow and gloom?"

He sat down to think, and as he thought, his heart grew lighter, and something almost like a smile came over his face. "I'll try it," he said to himself, as he rose from the rock on which he had been sitting and went towards home.

And this was what King Leo had been thinking: Have I ever done anything to make them care for me? They crowned me their king, but all my reign I have governed through fear. My roars were as mighty as the thunder; my will was hard and cruel. For a trifling offence

I have taken their lives, and now I am reaping
my reward. If it is not too late, I will begin
again. Love, not fear, shall be my motto this
time, and perhaps some day my life will be full
of happiness, instead of woe and misery.

And poor King Leo did begin again, and although the struggle was hard and the time of
conquest long, he did prove himself victor at
last, and died at a very old age, loved and re-
spected by all the beasts of the forest, having
proved to them all that Love hath greater power
than Fear.

The Willful Young Gobbler.

MADAME TURKEY put on her shawl and bonnet
to go to hunt for the silliest young turkey about
the place, because that silly young turkey was
her son. He had been gone since early morning,
and what had kept him his mother could not
guess. Mother Turkey and her young offspring
lived on a great big farm, and had been a very
happy pair, but Mother Turkey was growing
anxious. The fields had become bare and yellow, the trees stood around them tall and leafless,

and this meant a most serious matter to the Turkey family—it meant that Thanksgiving Day
was drawing near, and Madame Turkey well
knew that perhaps this handsome young son of
hers might grace the table at some beautifully
prepared dinner. She had little fear for herself,
for she had grown old and tough, but such a
big, fat bird as the young gobbler would hardly
escape the farmer's notice. Well she remembered how, year after year, her children had
fallen victims to the farmer's axe, and she had
tried to show this great big son how day by day
he was running into danger. But talk seemed
to count for nothing, he did not heed his mother's
warning words, but ate freely of the yellow corn
and the handfuls of wheat that the farmer's wife
scattered temptingly before them, and of course
he grew fatter all the time.

Now, do you wonder that Madame Turkey put
on her bonnet and shawl to search for her head-
strong son? She did not have far to go, for she
met him coming home, his hands in his trousers'
pockets, and his head up in the air, looking as
though he knew neither fear nor danger. Once
more this good, thoughtful mother reasoned with
her foolish son, but he only laughed at her fears,

and told her not to worry about him, for no turkey on the place could run faster than he, and

he could easily escape the farmer should he choose him for his Thanksgiving dinner.

But old heads are often the wisest, and had this silly young gobbler only listened to his mother he might still be strutting around the barnyard, or perhaps wandering through the wheat field, picking up the full, ripe grains that he loved so dearly. The farmer one day, as he sauntered through the poultry-yard, spied this well-fed gobbler, and decided that no finer bird than he could be found, and before Mr. Turkey had time to run, he was firm in the farmer's clutches, and before many minutes his life was over. What a foolish bird he was, and how much better it would have been had he only listened to the words of warning from his good old mother.

The Bears and the Hive.

Hug and Squeeze were two fat little cubs, who lived with their grandmother. Their mother had been captured in a trap when they were little, tiny bears, and Mother Bruin had taken them to her home and cared for them ever since. Such times as she had with them—they seemed to have been born under an unlucky

star, and poor old Grandmother Bruin had her
hands full.   They had of course fallen victims
to the measles, and next to the whooping-cough,
and they would eat so many sweets that the
toothache was almost a daily visitor.   Grand-

mother Bruin used to shake her poor old head
until her stiffly starched cap with its large purple bow would slip away off over her ear. She
did want very much that they should be good
little bears, and she would talk to Hug and

Squeeze so earnestly that they would promise to
be ever so much better, and they really meant it
when they promised, but when mischief came
into their heads, like a good many little boys
and girls—they forgot.

Tommy Jones was the gardener's son, and
Tommy wanted very much to become rich. He
had been given some money one day in the fall
for gathering chestnuts for his master's children.
Tom was proud to have money of his own, and
tried and tried to think of some plan to make it
more. One day, as he passed a shop window, he
saw little boxes with honey in them for sale;
this put an idea into Tommy's head. He would
go home, build some hives, and when spring
came get a swarm of bees, and then he, too,
could have honey to sell. Tommy was a wise
little chap to settle on this plan, for the roses
grew in great profusion, the lilies and honey-
suckle made rich food for the bees, and the
buckwheat fields that gleamed so white and
beautiful had sweetness beyond measure for
these busy little food gatherers.

Well, spring came, and Tommy beamed with
delight upon the neatly built hives that were to
be the homes of the honey makers and the source

of his wealth. Then summer came, and the work went bravely on until the cones were dripping with the store of golden honey.

Now Hug and Squeeze had been growing all this while, and the spirit for adventure kept growing with them. One night Grandmother Bruin had put them to bed and bade them be good, obedient children. They lay very still until their grandmother had gone, and then, as quietly as mice they crept out of bed and stole cautiously away. Through the woods they scampered, wild with joy over their freedom. The road reached, they could not make up their minds where to go, but the apples in the gardener's yard had made such fine balls before that they decided to try a game once more. Off they trotted, reached the garden, but stopped with wonder when they saw numbers of queer looking houses standing side by side. They had never seen hives before, and knew nothing about the savage little creatures that lived inside.

"We will take one home," said Hug, "it will be fine to play with."

Ball was forgotten, and Hug shouldered the hive, while little Squeeze scampered along at his side. But they had not gone far when Hug felt a sharp pinch on his ear, then one on his arm, and then he began to feel as though he was being stabbed all over. The bees were not long in finding out Squeeze, and run as they might, the cubs could not escape their tormentors.

"They are in the box," said Squeeze, "throw it away, do."

Hug threw away the box, but the bees still held fast. The more the bears tried to get rid of them the closer they clung, and the deeper they drove their stings. What a dreadful time

they had getting rid of them, and what pitiful
sights they were when they reached home.

Their faces were so swollen that it was hard
to tell who they were. Their ears were as large
as two, and their poor paws were smarting as if
from a burn. They were almost afraid to go
home, for they knew they were to blame for all
their suffering, but they felt so very badly that
they decided they must go to grandmother for
help. For little bears are like little children;
when they get hurt, they always want to get
home right away. So off they trotted as fast as
possible, and grandmother was very kind to them
in their trouble; she did not punish them, for she
thought they had been well rewarded for their
disobedience and meddlesome ways, but as she
tucket them in bed once more, after spreading
mud on their swollen hands and faces, she leaned
over them and said: "Will you try to let this be
a lesson, and listen more carefully hereafter to
your old grandmother's advice?" I think the
little bears learned a lesson which lasted them all
their lives, for they lived a great many years in
their old home, and never again meddled with
what did not belong to them.

The Fox's Story.

TELL you a story, little chap? Well, what do you suppose an old fellow like grandfather can tell to please you and Bushy? It's something that happened when I was young, you want? Well, let me think. So many things happened then, for grandfather was a gay young fox. I guess I'll tell you first about the great fox hunt from the castle. The castle stood high upon a hill, and one fine day the lords and ladies met there, and mounted upon their beautiful horses, started through the forest, the hounds dashing back of them, in front of them, and all around them, for the hounds go along to scent the fox, you know. I was young then, and the sight was new to me, and very dazzling, and although I had heard of the danger, I liked the excitement and noise. It was a beautiful sight, for the men wore bright scarlet jackets, which the dark dresses of the ladies made look still brighter. My curiosity came near putting an end to me that day, for I watched and waited almost too long, and only the greatest cunning on my part made the hounds lose the scent, and then the fun was spoiled.

Tell you some more? I'll give you some advice this time. Beware of traps. Many a handsome, brave young fox has been too curious, and
has poked his paw into some queer looking ob-

RELATING HIS ADVENTURES.

ject which he has discovered, only to have his
little paw caught, and has so lost his freedom
forever.

There is something else you must remember,
and it is to have lots of patience. One time, when

your father and uncle were little chaps, I took them out to get our Thanksgiving dinner. I had seen some fat, young turkeys roosting in a pear tree, and I wanted one of them very badly. The

moon rose early that night, and when we reached the tree, there sat five as pretty birds as I ever saw, but I had not been sharp in measuring my distance, and they were far beyond our reach.

So there we stood, and waited and waited, not knowing what to do. "Let's go home," said your father. "Not without our dinner," said I. "But we can't reach them," he replied. "Boys," I said, "we can wait," and we did wait. We hid back of the barn until morning dawned, and when the turkeys flew down to hunt for some breakfast, one of them was doubtless very much surprised to find himself stowed away in a bag preparatory to taking a ride on my shoulder. It was patience that won the turkey, boys, for had we grown tired and gone away, we certainly would have lost our fine dinner.

The farmer is no friend of ours, you know, and the farmer who lived at Hillside was very hard on us. He and his boys were always setting traps to capture some venturesome fellow. One day during harvest time, when the fields were bright with golden grain, I started off in search of something to eat. I crept along cautiously until I espied a duck so round and fat that it made my mouth water to look at her. I tried to plan some way to capture her. This seemed almost impossible, for the farmer was close by, and right by his side I could see the shining barrel of his trusty old gun, and I knew, if he

caught sight of me, he would certainly kill me.
But the temptation was so great that I ventured
closer and closer, grabbed the duck, stuffed her
into the bag, and scampered away across the
fields as fast as I could run. It is not wise to be
so daring; caution is always better, and it was
only luck that saved me that time.

I want you to be brave, boys, but I want you
to be careful as well. Don't creep too far from
behind the tree when you are lying in wait for
frisky young rabbits. They are as sharp and
watchful as any fox I ever knew, and I have
known a great many. And now I think you have
had stories enough for one day, and I want my

afternoon nap. I picked up a delicious fat goose this morning, and if you are good boys you can have it all before you creep into your piney beds and fall asleep to dream sweet dreams of the jolly times that are in store for all happy young foxes. And here we see them fast asleep in their beds the bones of the goose scattered all around.

The Fox Hunt.

LITTLE TOBY TROTTER came home from school on Friday night, threw his books on the very top shelf of the cupboard, and exclaimed, "You can rest there, my friend, for two whole days. I have seen all I want of you for this week, and haven't I pegged at you these five days harder than I ever did in all my life?"

To be sure, Toby had a good reason for his hard work, which, of course, you would like to know. While Toby was finishing his bowl of porridge and milk at breakfast Monday morning, his big brother Bill came into the room. "Toby," said he, "if you'll come home on Friday night, and tell me you are head of your class, I'll take you for a fox hunt on Saturday."

To say Toby was pleased does not begin to express his feelings; he was wild with delight. "I'll do it, Billy," said he, "you see if I don't. I'll work day and night before I will miss that fox hunt." Bill chuckled to himself to see little Toby so wrapt up in his studies. "I like the youngster's determination at any rate," thought he. Toby's hard work gained the day, and he could hardly wait until Bill came home to tell him he had kept his part of the contract. Bill was ready to do his part also, so they started from home the next morning, followed by old Bowser, the dog. Bill carried the gun. Toby would have liked to carry one also, but Bill thought he was better off without it. The woods where the fox lived was some little distance from the boys' home, and Toby ran along by Billy's side chattering as merrily as a magpie. A neighbor's dog, seeing old Bowser, joined the party, but he soon grew tired and left them. If Bowser had grown old he had not forgotten his early training as a hunter, and he went straight to

work to discover the whereabouts of Mr. Fox.
He had a lively chase, here and there, in and
around, but at last he seemed to be satisfied, and
Billy, who had watched him, followed carefully.
It was just outside the woods that Bowser came
upon the fox. The fox saw the dog at about the
same time the dog saw him. With one great
leap Mr. Fox bounded over the fence, Bowser
after him. On they flew, leaving Bill and poor
little Toby far behind them.

Bowser did his best, and just as he thought the
fox was his, the sly old fellow gave one swift
turn, darted into a deep hole in the ground, and
left poor old Bowser looking the picture of sorrowful defeat. The fox was lost, but Toby still
thought he had never known such sport in his
life, and he coaxed his brother to take him again
the next week. Bill said that just as long as
Toby would stand at the head of his class he
would take him every Saturday.

The Ride in the Balloon.

FOURTH of July dawned bright and smiling upon the little village of Browmew. Everywhere the flags were flying in honor of the glad

day and long streamers of red, white and blue bunting floated gaily to the breeze. The young people, roused from their slumbers by the bang-ing of the cannon, hurried into the streets to celebrate this glorious day. The youths had donned their best suits, and all the happy young girls had bedecked themselves in the most charming style. Miss Kitty Stripe, the belle of the village, won the admiration of all, for where could one find a sweeter creature than she? Her soft, pretty ears were tied with the loveliest pink ribbon, and the waving plume in her hat exactly matched the ribbon in color. Quite proud Foxy Terry felt as he walked by her side that fine morning.

Fireworks blazed all day. It is true that Spitzy White burnt all the hair off his pretty little face, and little Mattie Gray had her ear shot off by a pistol, but they did not mind such little accidents, and all agreed that the fireworks were quite a success.

The great event of the day, however, was to be the balloon ascension. Never had such an event been heard of in Browmew. All the folks turned out to see it. Old Tortoise Shell came, although he was as blind as a bat, for he declared that it made him feel young again to hear the cheering. Foxy Terry and Kitty Stripe had agreed to take the ride. About four o'clock the

balloon was brought out, and ere long all was in
readiness, and they had stepped into the basket

and were rising from the earth. Cheer after
cheer went up as they left the ground. Up, up
they sailed. Over roofs and steeples they rose,
until it seemed to the crowd below that they
would never stop. They rose so high that the
ropes got tangled on the horn of the moon,
which they had not been able to avoid, since
they could not see it on account of the bright
sunshine. Poor Pussy was greatly terrified, but
brave Foxy bids her be patient, and he will set
matters right. He soon manages to get the balloon free, and slowly they begin to descend. The
ride is a short one, but it satisfies Miss Kitty, and
she is glad to come down. When they reach the
ground, they are greeted with outstretched arms
and praised for their bravery. So the day ends
amid general rejoicing, and at a late hour all the
sleepy young folks crawl into bed to dream of
the sports of the day, and to look forward with
pleasure to the next year, when they should be
able to have another good time together on the
green.

Lessons for Young Foxies.

Mrs. Ruby Bush was really a very handsome young fox—the handsomest in the whole neighborhood, so it was said, and they said, too, how good and gentle she was, which was lots better

than being called beautiful, for kindness goes a great deal farther than good looks.

She and her husband and her two little ones lived in the "Tall Tree" forest as happy and loving a family as the sun ever shone upon. The two little foxes, Vic and Vim, played together all day. They had the finest games of hide and go seek, the great holes in the trunk of the old oak tree making the jolliest kind of hiding places. They pulled the tiny flowers that grew in the woods, and made wreaths and bouquets to carry home to Mother Bush. Life was just one long play day to them. Ruby Bush was a good little mother, and she wanted to see her boys well brought up, so the time came when she thought it best to give them a lesson in hunting.

The moon was new, but the night was clear and the stars twinkled brightly. Vic had his turn first, and he and his mother started off to the nearest poultry yard, each carrying a long white bag.

The turkeys were roosting on the top of a rail fence, not dreaming of any danger, and Mother Fox and Vic had little trouble to fill their bags. Vic was much pleased over his success, and thought it almost as much fun as playing with Vim.

Father Bush had seen a trap in the forest, and had told his wife about it. "Now," thought she, is the time to teach my boys of the danger of traps." So, when the boys started off to play, as usual, she called them back, telling them she wanted them to go with her as she had something to show them. The trap was near their home, and the boys gazed in wonder at this strange object, and listened with interest to the

tales their mother told of its great dangers. A delicious piece of meat had been used for bait, and Vic and Vim and Mother Bush, too, wished they might have it. To wish meant to try with Mother Bush, so she got a long stick, and telling her boys to keep away, carefully pried open the trap and drew out the treasure. What a fine time they had eating it and wishing they could find another!

The Hunter Treed.

For two or three weeks old Jack Frost had been at work in the forest, pinching the leaves from the trees, and sending the ripe nuts to the ground. Great piles of leaves, that Nature's

artist had painted brown and red, gold and crimson, lay on the ground, making a soft, thick carpet for the dwellers of the forest.

In this forest, the Bear, the Wolf and the Fox lived, and three greater cronies you never heard

of.   The Bear was the oldest and the biggest,
but little Foxy always led the fun, for he was
one of the brightest, smartest little chaps that
ever dwelt in the forest.   Through the fallen

leaves he came tramping one day to the house
of neighbor Bear, and with his usual cheery
"How-do-you-do?" greeted his friend.   He had
heard that much mischief was being done by a

cruel, hard-hearted hunter, and he wanted the
Bear and their friend, the Wolf, go with him
and try to put an end to the hunter's fun. They
went to the Wolf's house, and found him willing
to help, so side by side they started through the
woods. Nothing happened for some time, but
finally the sharp ears of little Foxy heard the
sound of a gun in the distance. Bidding his
friends be quiet, he waited until it sounded
again. This time Foxy learned the direction
from which it came, and they hurried on toward
the spot. Bang, bang, bang! The gun kept
sounding louder and louder as they sped along.
Now a new noise greeted their ears. It sounded
like the chattering of many voices, and as they
turned the corner they came upon a strange
sight. Up in the tree that bore but one branch
and must at one time have been struck by light-
ning, hung the cruel hunter, while below him
on the ground danced and played a greedy crowd
of wolves. One had his empty gun, two more
were fighting for his hat, and the rest stood
barking at the hunter in the wildest manner.
The three cronies were too late to carry out their
scheme, but they laughed merrily over the victory of the others, and they were greatly pleased

that at last they were to be set free from the
danger in which they had been so long, and

The Hunter treed.

could now roam over the forest at their pleasure
without fear of being killed by the hunter's gun.
The poor fellow in the tree was in a very un-

comfortable position, as we can well see, and he
was in constant fear lest the wolves, in some
way, might be able to reach him. He saw no
way in which he could escape, and felt sure that
his time to die had at last come. He hoped the
wolves would be attracted by something else, and
go away and leave him, but that seemed to be
almost too good a fortune. The wolves kept the
poor man in the tree until they heard the sound
of approaching footsteps and caught the sounds
of frequently fired guns; then they all scampered
away as fast as possible, and then the poor man
was rescued by his friends, who had come in
search of him.

The three friends were very much disappointed when their victim escaped, but they
hoped he would be so badly frightened that he
would, in the future, keep away from the forest,
and so far as we know he never troubled them
again.

The Lost Dinner.

"COME, my dear," said Mrs. Fox, as she
pinned her plaid shawl around her shoulders and
tied on her bonnet that was trimmed with one

of the sun-flowers she had gathered from the
kitchen garden that morning, "if you'll be a very

good little boy, and promise not to get in the way, you may go to market with me. I have noticed for several evenings past that a fat young gobbler roosts on the fence that is built along the road. This is too good a prize to lose, my dear, and he shall be mine to-night. If I am not as young as I used to be, I have not forgotten the art of bagging game, and it will be well for you, my child, if you keep your eyes open and try to profit by my example."

"Indeed, mother," said young Rufus," you will find me just as good as can be, and I am sure no one could be a better teacher than you, for well I remember the good dinners you have brought home from the farm-yard."

The roadside and the rail fence were soon gained, and in less time than it takes to tell it, Mr. Gobbler had found a place inside Mother Fox's basket, and the lid was shut down tight.

"Oh dear me!" thought the poor turkey, "why was I so foolish as to roost on that rail fence? If I had only listened to my mother's warning, what a happy turkey I might still be; but I thought I was old enough and smart enough to take care of myself. If I could only get out I'd be so careful hereafter." But the lid was shut

down tight, and there seemed no chance for the
gobbler.

Mother Fox and Rufus chatted merrily as
they trotted along, and when they came to the
rail fence along the edge of the woods, Rufus
begged they might stop and rest awhile, for the
sharp stones had hurt his feet.

Up they scrambled, and seated themselves
quite happily, and Rufus laughed merrily as his
mother told him of the many times she had
escaped the hunter's dogs, and he listened with
a very grave face as she talked to him of the
traps and snares the farmers set to catch the fox
who was foolish enough to go near them.

Mother Fox became so interested in her lesson
that she quite forgot the turkey in the basket,
but all of a sudden he gave one frantic lurch,
and over went Mother Fox's basket and its precious contents. Mother Fox was quick, but the
gobbler was quicker—out of the basket he
popped under the fence, and away he hurried as
fast as his legs could carry him. After him came
the fox; nearer and nearer she came, so close
now that she grabbed his tail feathers, but they
yielded to her clutch, and the turkey hurried
on. On, on he went, until at last, with one
mighty effort, one tremenduous flapping of
wings, he reached the wagon-house roof, tremb-

ling and exhausted, but having left the fox below.

This was a hard lesson for the gobbler, but it
was a good one, and never again did any one
hear of that turkey roosting on a fence rail. He
did not wish to run any more chances of getting
into the clutches of the wily old fox.

The New Spring Suit.

SPRING had come again. Spring, warm and
gentle—not March with its howling winds pinching your noses and fingers and toes, and bidding
the big round tears to chase each other down
your poor little faces. The warm April showers
told that spring had come. As the rain pattered
down upon the earth, softening the hard crust of
winter, up popped the little faces of the snow-
drop and daffodils, crocuses opened their eyes to
the bright golden sun, and the tulips put on
their robes of crimson and yellow to tell of
spring's arrival.

While nature was putting on her new and
beautiful apparel, Mr. Rufus Cunning began to

open his eyes and wonder if it was not about time for him to think of his spring costume.

Now one of Rufus' great failings was his love for dress. It is a fact, though a very sorry one, that nearly all his time and thoughts were spent in planning what would be the most becoming style of clothing.

Off he started one fine morning to fit himself out with a rig most charming. First of all he visited the tailor and bought of him a suit which he considered quite a beauty. His linen was the next purchase, and the collar he chose was so high that one would pity him, did he not think him so very foolish to suffer thus for show. But people who are older and wiser than this gay young fox do just such silly things.

His next stop was at the boot-maker's. Mr. Shoemaker never in all his life found anybody so hard to please, but at last a pair was found to suit him, and then a hat must be gotten. Hat after hat was tried on, but by and by a hat, tall and black and shiny, met Foxy's view, and his eyes danced with pleasure as he gazed at himself in the mirror. Now all was complete except the gloves—these were not hard to find, and then he started for home. You should have seen this

vain young creature as he walked along the street
—everything complete, from the crown of his
head to the soles of his feet—not even the walk-
ing-stick, nor the eye-glass had been forgotten.
If no one admired his fine appearance, Foxy was
happy in the entire satisfaction he felt in himself.

But alas, alas! he had just taken his friend,
Miss Bruin, out for a little stroll, when the worst
shower of the whole season came up. You
should have seen them run, when the first large
drops came pattering down. There seemed to
be no shelter near at hand, and they were getting
pretty wet, when Miss Bruin spied some old
friends gathered under an old umbrella, which
little Floy, the pet of the household, had left in
the woods the day before. So Foxy and she
made a dash for this refuge and reached it just
as the rain began to pour down in torrents. They
were pretty well crowded, but they were very
thankful to have even that much protection, and
they really enjoyed themselves chatting with
their friends. The shower lasted only a few
minutes, and when it was over they started for
home, as it was too wet to go farther and Foxy
was very much worried over his new rig, which
was nearly ruined.

Monkey Jack.

UNCLE MAC had been away for years in South America, mother told us children, and South America became the extent of travel, the most remote corner of the world, to our childish

minds. How we listened with the keenest interest to the occasional letters which arrived, and how we wondered what this far-away uncle was like, for Rob and I were but babies when he went away. One night, I can remember it just perfectly, although I was only a mite of a girl, we were gathered around the open fire in the library, for the September nights were chilly, when the maid announced a gentleman in the parlor. He gave no name, but said he knew he would be welcome. Mother left us, but in almost no time we heard her calling, "Children, children, come quickly, your Uncle Mac is home!" Rob and I pranced down like little ponies, and were almost smothered in this big uncle's arms. After the first welcome had been given, uncle asked if he might bring in his traveling companion, for he was sure he must be tired of being alone so long. We children wondered why the poor traveler had been left in the hall, but all wonderment was dispelled when a sleepy, sorrowful looking monkey appeared in uncle's arms. Oh! how wild Rob was with delight. I was rather timid and kept at a distance.

Before Rob had finished admiring this funny little chap, Nan, the nurse, came to take him off to bed. I am sorry to say that Rob was not a bit good, but screamed dreadfully, until uncle told him that if he would stop crying, Jack, as he called the monkey, might sleep in his room. Mother shook her finger reprovingly at Uncle

Mac, but I heard him whisper that he must be humored his first night at home. I followed Rob and Nan, and how I did laugh when I saw Jack lie down on the quilt Nan put in the corner, and nestle his head down on his hand. Such a poor, sleepy monkey as he was!

But this state of serenity was not to last long. Early in the morning, before daybreak, Nan was wakened by a tremendous clatter, and jumped up to find that Master Jack had stripped the walls of pictures, and was preparing to divest the bureau of any ornaments. Nan captured him and tied him to the foot-board of the bed; but just as her sleepy eyes had closed for a good, long nap, a scream from Rob aroused her, and she found that naughty monkey amusing himself by vigorously pulling Rob's hair. "No more peace for me," thought Nan, so she dressed as quickly as possible, and carried Jack down into the garden.

How soon we grew attached to the little fellow, for he was so bright and full of cunning tricks. It was very amusing to watch him take his funny little hands and with his thumb and middle finger knock the ashes from Uncle Mac's cigar. He was very fond of hard boiled eggs, and if we gave one to him hot, he would throw it from hand to hand until it became cool, and then with his clever little fingers he would remove the shell just as daintily as possible. Another favorite dish of his was red raspberries;

black he would not touch. One day the cook gave him some red berries in a china saucer, and determined to keep her eyes upon him, as he had no regard for crockery. Something demanded her attention, and she forgot the mon-

key until a gentle tap on the step attracted her
attention, and there stood Jack, holding his plate
towards her for more.

We kept Jack for several years; but one time,
while we were away in the country, the poor
little fellow met with an accident that caused his
death. Rob grieved very much after his queer
play-fellow, and declared that he could never
again love an animal as he did that monkey. I
guess we all felt sad over his loss, for we liked
the cunning chap and missed his cute and funny
capers.

The Meeting on the Bridge.

IF you'll go through the woods for about a
quarter of a mile, and then turn to the right, you
will find a bridge, which is formed from rocks
against which the waters trickled untiringly year
after year, until quite an opening was made, and
now the little stream flows on day after day, singing its low, sweet song. If you'll follow this
tiny stream you will see it growing broader and
broader, until at last it becomes a large and

beautiful river.   But our story is about the bridge over the little stream, and what happened there.

One morning the elephant dressed himself in his very best, put on his tall white hat, took his stick in his hand, and started through the woods to visit his friend, the giraffe. He took his time, for the day was warm, and he liked to listen to the birds and watch the gentle rustle of the leaves as the soft wind shook them.

He was surprised when he looked at the sun and found that the morning was fast drawing to a close. He walked on much faster than was comfortable, and his temper was not the sweetest when he came to the bridge and found the donkey standing on it watching the waters flow over the rocks.

"Move on, my friend," said the elephant, "this is no place for halting."   But the donkey was not pleased to be spoken to in this manner, and he made no effort to move. On the bridge stepped the elephant, but still the donkey did not stir.

"Perhaps you did not hear me," said the elephant. "I told you to move on."

"Quite plainly I heard you," replied the don-

key, "but it does not please me to stir from this spot."

Both the elephant and the donkey were growing angrier every minute. At last the elephant, who, of course, was lots the larger, picked up the donkey with his trunk, and dipped him up and down in the cool stream until he cried for mercy. If the sun was hot, the water was cool, and this sudden plunge was certainly not to the donkey's liking, and his wild struggles afforded the elephant much amusement. As he stepped back, laughing at the donkey's frantic efforts, his foot slipped, and over he went, splash, into the water. The water was not very deep, and they soon scrambled to the shore, but both had learned a lesson, and before parting they decided that the better plan was to yield to one another. Had the elephant spoken in a kindly manner, and had the donkey been more accommodating, each might have escaped a most unpleasant experience.

The elephant's bath had left him in no condition for calling, and his tall white hat he prized so much had gone floating down the stream, but he did not grumble, for he knew the fault was his own. He felt that he might have avoided this very unpleasant ending to the happy time he had had in prospect, if he had only remembered to be a little more polite. As he journeyed through the woods once more he was a wise elephant, if, as my be imagined, a sadder one.

The Runaway Pair.

LITTLE RHODY GRAY was trembling like a leaf —not because Jack Frost was teasing her ratship, no indeed. The grass was green, and the beautiful little wild flowers held up their heads to say "good-night" before they closed their drowsy eyes. The air was soft and balmy, whispering secrets, low and sweet, as it stole quietly in and out through the tree tops. But Rhody was trembling, and it was fear that made her, for she was sure some one would see her, crouching down behind the lilac bush at the end of the garden.

How bright the moon was growing. Rhody thought she had never seen it so dazzlingly large before. It seemed as though it were looking right down upon her, showing every one where the timid little rat was hiding. Now Rhody was waiting for some one—and this some one was

Jacky Leap—just the handsomest, largest frog in the whole pond.

He and Rhody had planned to leave the old place that night and go off and be married.

They were both young and wilful lovers, and because Mother Gray had said no when Jack asked for Rhody, they had made up their minds to have their own way, come what would. Now then, do you wonder that Rhody was frightened?

It was growing so late that she felt sure Jack had forgotten her, and her little heart went thumpty-bang! until she was certain some one would hear it. Poor foolish Rhody, it only sounded so loud to her ears. But at last she caught sight of some gleaming white object almost flying towards her, and what should it be but the white rabbit that had been bought at Easter for the baby at the house. Jack had told Bun of their plans, and he had promised to help them—and he certainly did. Jack was seated on his back, such a big, broad, furry back, and Rhody was soon mounted behind her lover. How they flew along! Fences and trees seemed to dash past them. Poor little frightened Rhody held on with all her might, fearing every minute that she might slip off and be left behind, until at last they came to the hollow tree where the wise old owl lived.

He blinked at them through his spectacles, but asked no questions, and in less than no time Rhody was Mrs. Leap. Bun was waiting for them, and they mounted once more and started for home. It was hard to tell Mother Gray what they had done—but she was a kind old rat, and concluded that the only way was to make the best of things, so she gave them her blessings, and Jack and his little wife Rhody were as happy a couple as lived in the Green.

Chanty's Lesson.

"Cock a doodle doo!" shrilly crowed Mr.
Chanticleer as he strutted around in the barnyard. Chanty had just learned to crow, and he
was as proud as any rooster could be over his
own voice. He was not a very beautiful bird,

for his tail feathers had just commenced to grow,
and his legs were so long and thin you wanted
to laugh at him, if that had not been the rudest
thing you could possibly do. But still, one could

not help thinking him a very foolish fellow as
he watched him strutting around, as though he
owned the barnyard. But grief, you know sometimes comes to people who think themselves so
far above their neighbors; so listen to the narrow
escape that Chanty had one summer evening.

Down in the woods, not far away from the
home of Chanty, lived a smart red fox; he was
young and called a very handsome fellow, and
old Mother Fox smiled with approval when she
saw her son going off rigged in his finest suit, his
hat perched on one side, with a turkey feather
sticking in it, and his sharp pointed knife shining in his belt.

One night this young fox bade good-bye to
his mother, gathered up the bag that always
hung back of the door, and started off towards
the farm-yard. You can guess his purpose, perhaps—Chanty's shrill crow had reached his ears,
and he made up his mind in an instant that he
would like the rooster in a pot-pie much better
than strutting around the barnyard.

Fate had been kind to Chanty this time, and
when Master Fox reached the place, all he could
see of the rooster was his tail feathers sticking
through the stable door, and the farmer's man

had made the door fast with lock and key. The
fox grabbed the tail feathers, but Chanty was
safe, though woefully frightened, and, we hope,
wiser, content to go his way through life without making himself so evident.

Fido, the Shepherd Dog.

FIDO was a tiny black pup when he came to
live on the farm. He was born in a great big
place, called a kennel, where lots of other dogs
lived. One day, just after he had finished his
saucer of milk and had made up his mind to enjoy a good long nap, a boy, who was always
poking around where he was not wanted, came,
and with no gentle hand grabbed him up and
carried him far away from the other dogs. Fido
shut his eyes and growled, as he thought, quite
savagely. Then he heard the boy say, "This is
a beauty, and I can promise you he will turn out
a fine dog." Somebody took him away from the
boy then, and Fido liked the way he stroked his
head, so gentle, and called him "a pretty little
fellow," and he liked the pleasant way in which

this somebody laughed when he, Fido, began
licking his hand.

"I'll take him," he heard the stranger say, and

then, without another word, Fido was tucked
away into the pocket of the man's great coat. It
seemed such a long while to Fido before he
heard the farmer say "Whoa" to his horses, and

then he heard a little childish voice say, "Did you bring him, Father?" and Fido knew she meant him, for the farmer reached into his pocket, hauled him out, and replied, "Here he is, little Nan; give him something to eat, for he must be hungry after his long ride."

"Oh, Father, what a darling he is," and she hugged Fido so tight that he really had to squeal to himself from being choked to death. Little Nan could hardly allow Fido time to lap his milk, she was so wild with delight over him, and when he had finished she gathered him in her chubby arms and rocked him just as she had seen mother rock the baby, singing to him softly one of baby's bye-low songs. Fido felt so happy that it was not long before he was sound asleep and snoring like a good fellow. When mother called Nan to go to bed, she put Fido in the box that father had built for him, and Fido was so sleepy he could hardly wag his curly tail to show his pleasure.

The next morning Fido wakened bright and early, and gazed with wonder at the new world into which he had come. Nan brought him his breakfast of bread and milk, and then off they started for a jolly scamper. Such fun as these

two had together. Wherever Nan went, Fido
followed, and Nan was such a kind, loving little
mistress that he loved her dearly.

Fido grew bigger and stronger every day, and
he certainly made good the boy's promise of his
becoming a fine dog. He found out by and by
that life was not all play, for the farmer carried
him off one day to teach him to mind the sheep.
It was not long before Fido knew all about it,
and the farmer told little Nan that he was the
best shepherd dog he had ever had.

Now the old wolf, who lived in the woods
back of the pasture lot, had found out what a
good shepherd Fido was, for try as he might,
not once could he find him napping. One day
this wolf thought he would be very cunning and
get the best of Fido, so he went carefully out to
the corn field one night, and robbed the scare-
crow of his clothes and rigged himself in them,
thinking that Fido would not know him.

The moon was shining brightly, and as the
wolf came across the field, Fido pricked up his
ears and looked at him suspiciously. He knew
that he did not belong in the field any way, and
so he kept pretty close watch over him. Closer
and closer came the wolf, and Fido waited

quietly for him, and then, with one long, knowing look, leaped upon him. It was too bad, but
Fido had grabbed the coat and not the wolf, so
that Mr. Wolf slipped out of his covering and

was off in the woods as fast as his legs could
carry him, and never again, as far as we know,
has he tried to play any tricks on Fido.

But for Fido, Nan's father might have lost

many of his valuable sheep, and he could not be grateful enough to the faithful dog for his good service.

Nan was very proud of her Fido when her father told of the way in which he looked after the flock, and said she was quite sure nothing would ever harm them as long as he was around.

Quite often Fido would go with Nan's father, and help him drive his sheep to market, and he was always so faithful and trusty that Nan's father was never sorry that he stopped that day and got the little fellow.

The Bicycle Race.

THE glorious Fourth had proclaimed itself all day long. Bang! Bang! Bang! went the cannons, Bang! Bang! Bang! echoed the crackers, and Bang! Bang! Bang! sounded the torpedoes small and great. Gunpowder made the air heavy and oppressive, and the clouds gathering in the sky made one very uncertain as to whether or not the rain would put an end to all the fun. Large posters in red and blue letters had notified the people that the most beautiful fireworks they had ever seen would be put off back of the Grove house—so do you wonder that the sky was watched most anxiously?

Now the people of the town were not alone in wishing for a clear night. The young folks who dwelt in the woods were watching the clouds with just the keenest interest, even the tiniest speck of blue sky was hailed with shouts of delight. Were they, too, going to celebrate this day of Independence? Why, to be sure they were. They were not going to send off rockets and bombs. Roman candles and pin-wheels were not part of their fun. These forest folks had invited all their friends to witness a bicycle race. The bear, the wolf, the fox, the rabbit, the porcupine and the catamount were to take part, and as no bicycle race had ever been ridden in these parts, the greatest interest was taken in it by all the animals in the country round.

For weeks they had been practicing. Early and late you might see these four-footed fellows mounted on their wheels, and pushing them along just as fast as ever they could. It was not all fun either, for tires would slip off the rims, nuts constantly became loose, and sometimes it happened that a stone or a twig or something of

the sort sent the rider off his wheel, and then
bent handle-bars must be straightened, or worse
still, bruised heads must be tied up—but all
these woes were part of the undertaking, so no
one dared complain, but must go to work and try
again.

Well, all these trials were over now, and the
evening had come when fate should decide to
whom the honor belonged. What a crowd had
gathered to see them. The squirrels sat chattering together up in the trees; the crickets and
katy-dids tried to outdo each other in their lively
chirrup, and the nightingale raised her sweet
voice and poured forth the loveliest music.

One! two! three! croaked the frog, and off
they started. The rabbit was first. "Three
cheers for Bun!" shouted the crowd. "Bruin is
ahead! Three cheers for Bruin." "It's the Fox
this time!" "No, he has lost his place, Bruin is
ahead again!" "Oh, what a shame, the wolf has
fallen off! No use trying again, poor wolf, the
others are far ahead."

First it was one and then another, until at last,
just as the goal was reached, little Bun with one
mighty effort came in first. How the crowd
cheered, and what a happy fellow Bun was. It

was hard for the others, but as some one must win, all felt satisfied that it should be the little rabbit. Then the lion, who was judge, awarded the prize, which was the nicest bicycle ever made, and little Bun went home very happy.

The Jolly Chinee.

WE WO WANG was a "Jolly Chinee." From the time he opened his funny almond-shaped eyes in the morning until sleep closed them for him at night, he laughed and chatted, and sang the merriest kind of songs. He liked the sun, because it always seemed so bright and happy— he loved to be out in it. He liked all sorts of flowers, the gayer the better for him; he liked his clothes the brightest; everything must be brilliant and sparkling to please We Wo Wang, the "Jolly Chinee."

We Wo Wang had two sisters, who had funny almond-shaped eyes just like his, and long, straight, black hair, like his also. But they did not wear a pigtail as We Wo Wang did; they piled their hair on top of their heads, and dressed it beautifully, they thought, with fancy pins and

tiny fans. They wore queer little shoes, that
were so tight they pinched their toes dreadfully,
and made them sway from side to side as they
walked along. One day We Wo Wang said to
his sisters, "My dears, I am sure, if I tried I

might walk down
those balusters. I
think I might do
it gracefully, too; I
know just how I
would balance my-
self." His sisters
were horrified at the
idea, and begged him not
to try, but We Wo Wang
was determined. He mount-
ed the rail, opened his fan,

fluttered it from side to side, and commenced the descent.

The servants hearing of their master's doings, hurried from all parts of the house to see the sight. But alas! for poor We Wo Wang; his foot slipped, and he came crashing down to the floor. Away flew his hat, away flew his fan. Servants rushed to pick him up, and his two little sisters came hobbling down the stairs as fast as ever they could, expecting to see We Wo Wang battered to pieces. There were no bones broken, and arnica and court plaster soon made him pretty comfortable. But there was something hurt past healing, and that was We Wo Wang's pride. It grieved him to think his servants had seen his failure. It was bad enough for his sisters to have been witnesses, but it was dreadful to have these chattering servants laugh and joke over his downfall. He made up his mind to punish them for having so much curiosity, so he had one of them carry him into the hall, prop him up with pillows, and then he ordered them to walk down the ballusters, one after the other, while he sat and watched their defeat just as they had witnessed his. The servants were greatly terrified when they heard this command, but of course they all had to try, because they dared not disobey their master's

command. One after another they mounted the stairs, and took their positions to descend, but

not in the way We Wo Wang intended. Off
they tumbled, one after another, bruising their
poor bodies and wishing they had kept out of the
way, and not been so curious. We Li Ho came
very near coming down in safety, but near the
bottom his foot slipped, and he too fell down.
As We Wo Wang sat and watched them, he
laughed hard enough to split his sides, for no
one was able to accomplish the feat.

A Chinese Adventure.

WE WING WO was a little yellow Chinaman.
He belonged to one of the best families, as any
one could tell from his red and yellow girdle.
That he never worked a day in his life might also
be told by the great length of his finger nails, of
which he was wonderfully proud. He was also
proud of his round, plump figure, for Chinamen,
you know, like to be fat. Like the rest of his
countrymen, he had almond-shaped eyes, and
wore his shiny black hair in a long, carefully
combed pig-tail.

We Wing Wo was very fond of good things

to eat, and he thought no one could cook these good things as well as his servant, Ho Che Lee.

How old We Wing Wo would smile with delight when the bird's-nest soup was set before

him; and then, again, how merrily he would
chuckle over a dish of shark's fins or deer's
sinews, and the never-forgotten pearly white
rice! We Wing Wo could make his chop sticks
fly when all these dainties graced his table. But
above all things, We Wing Wo loved a cup of
good, strong tea. It seemed to drive away all
cares and troubles. Ho Che Lee always kept
some ready in a funny brown tea-pot.

We Wing Wo had never been to sea, and he
was siezed with a wild desire to try a trip on the
briny deep. One day he called his faithful Ho
Che Lee to him, and telling him his wish, bade
him pack a hamper with eatables, hunt up a
boat, and prepare to take the journey with him.
Poor Ho Che Lee shook with fear at such a
prospect, but he dared not question his master's
order, and so went away to do his bidding.
When all was ready, Ho Che Lee suggested that
it might be better to take with them somebody
who knew a thirg or two about a boat. We
Wing Wo agreed to this; a fellow was found,
and the three set sail.

All went well at first, but by and by poor We
Wing Wo wished he was on shore, for he was
growing sicker every minute.

"Let's go home," said he.   "Sailing is no pleasure at all."

It was easy enough to say, go home, but try as they might, neither the sailor nor He Che Lee could manage the boat.

"Throw out a line," said We Wing Wo, "and see how deep it is." Out went the line, and out went luckless Lee; not to drown, however, for after much pulling he was landed safely in the boat.

How all of them longed for shore, and how very small their chances of getting there did seem! But fate is sometimes kind, and so she proved herself this time.

Some men had been watching the boat from the shore, and had seen the poor fellows' sorry plight; so they tied a rope round the waist of one good-hearted Chinaman, and sent him to the rescue. He swam out to them, fastened the rope to the bow, and with many long, strong pulls We Wing Wo was hauled to shore.

The Eagle's Christmas.

On the top of a high mountain a mother eagle had built a nice, soft nest. She did not build where some eagles do, in the cleft of the rocks, but in top of a large tree. In the nest she laid four eggs, and there, day after day, she sat on the nest, keeping the eggs warm, until one day she heard a gentle rap-rap against the shell. The knocking grew louder and louder, and a bit of the shell fell off the end of the egg, and slowly a little head came out, and then a little body, and in the course of a few hours the old Mother Eagle found herself with four little ones to look after. It kept her very busy indeed, supplying all their wants, and she had to make a good many trips to the valley to get them the food they wanted.

All babies must have a name, and so the old Mother Eagle put on her thinking cap, and tried to find a name for each child; but, like all mammas, none was good enough. At last she decided to call them Tim, Sam, Chirp and Baldy.

They were a funny looking lot of creatures, to be sure, with their big heads, and mouths always open, and we would not think them at all pretty; but they seemed beautiful to their mamma, and she was always trying to think up ways of making them happy. No children ever spent more happy days than these little eagles. Strange to say, they never quarreled. If Sam felt cross, and was likely to scold, the other little ones would creep away, and leave him to himself until he was good-natured once more. They loved one another very dearly, and each one was ready to do as the others wished. They never said, "I won't play, if you do that," as some little boys and girls do.

They were still quite young, so young that they had not yet learned to fly, when the glad Christmas time rolled around. The snow had been falling for several days, and the mountain tops were covered with a beautiful white blanket. On the fir trees just near the eagle's nest, the snow glistened like diamonds in the morning sun. Sam and Tim, Baldy and Chirp were up early that Christmas morning, for, like all little folks, they wanted to see if Santa Claus had brought them anything. All the week they had been wild with excitement, for, although they had never had a Christmas, their mamma had told them all about it, and it seemed as if they could never wait for the day to come. Each tiny eagle had written down just what he wanted, and mamma had a long list when she started off that morning to get the gifts and the Christmas dinner. Santa Claus was so busy supplying the wants of the children down in the valley, that he did not have time to visit the nest, but he met the Mother Eagle one day as he was driving over the mountain, and he had promised to leave a lot of nice toys for the little ones hidden in the hollow tree at the foot of the mountain, where she could get them. Santa Claus has such a good, kind heart that he could not bear to think that even little eagles should be forgotten on this glad day, when all of God's creatures should be happy.

All day the little eagles sat on the branches of the tree which was their home, craning their long necks and straining their eyes to catch the first sight of their mother as she flew homeward. They did not even take time for their mid-day nap, and if they had not been so anxious to see what their mamma would bring, I fear they would have dropped asleep and perhaps would have fallen out of the tree to the ground below. It was nearly twilight when the mother came home, and how joyfully the little ones greeted her, and how delighted they were with her well-filled basket. They chattered and chirped in their own language until their poor mother was almost wild with their noise, but she was also very much pleased to see them all so happy.

What a nice Christmas dinner they had. True, their turkey was not roasted or garnished, as ours is, but they liked it all the better. First there was the nicest, sweetest fish you ever saw, served up in true eagle style. Then a nice rabbit, two young pigeons and some fat ducks. When the youngsters had finished their dinner, their mamma brought out a bag of yellow corn and a lot of rosy cheeked apples, which she had stolen from a farmer's wagon. My, how those little eagles did eat. It was a great wonder they did not all die.

When the feast was over, and the horns and drums, the bright picture books, and the other pretty toys were distributed, they all decided that Christmas was the happiest time imaginable. "Well, really," said little Baldy, "I wish Christmas came oftener." And all the others cried, "So do we."

Tale of the Ostrich Hunter.

DID you ever hear of a bird that could not fly? That seems odd, does it not? But a bird, called the ostrich, belongs to this family. Its wings are so tiny that they are of little use to him, except that while running they spread out and catch the air. If the ostrich has not the power of flying, which other birds possess, he is gifted with the ability to run at a wonderfully swift pace. To help him in this direction, he is provided with strong, long legs, that carry him across the country as rapidly as the swiftest horse. The long neck of this bird is covered with soft, downy plumage, but its body is covered with the beautiful, graceful plumes that are used for trimming our hats and bonnets.

The home of the ostrich is in the hot, sunny desert land of Africa. It is a very tall bird, measuring six feet, and sometimes eight. Its food is principally grass and grains, but it picks up and devours sand and pieces of stone and bone. It will also eat insects, small birds and snakes. Large numbers of them will feed together; in fact, they live in flocks, often of great size. The mother bird, before laying her eggs, scratches a hole in the ground, thus making her nest. She lays ten or twelve eggs in the same

place. In the daytime she allows the heat of the sun to hatch them, but at night she sits on them and keeps them warm. These eggs are said to weigh three pounds apiece and to be good to eat. The father ostrich sometimes grows weary of the long term of hatching, and breaks the eggs before the tiny bird is ready to come out.

The feathers of the ostrich are worth a great deal of money. Sometimes the birds are hunted by natives on horseback, and the horses are trained for this long, tedious ride for a great while—the bird is not easily caught by its pursuer.

There are farms, called ostrich farms, where the birds are raised in great numbers. The eggs are set, and the baby ostriches hatched, watched and cared for until they are old enough to yield the beautiful plumage.

If the ostrich is taken away from its home and put in a cage, it will in time become quite tame and gentle toward those to whom it is used, but it does not like a stranger, and if it gets a chance will knock him down and trample on him.

Somebody told a funny story about an old fellow, who thought he would take his gun and go hunting for ostriches, as he wanted to get a lot of nice feathers and some of the birds to send away to a museum. So he started out on the

desert to hunt his prey.   Pretty soon he came
upon an ostrich that was resting in the sun, and
raising his gun to his shoulder, he fired.   He
wounded the bird so that it could not walk very
fast, and thinking that he would be able to cap-

ture it, if he could wound it in such a manner as
to stop its walking, he crept carefully toward it,
and stooping down, attempted to cut off its leg
with his sharp, strong sword.   He felt quite sure
of his prize now, but had not counted on what
was going to happen.   The ostrich is a very wise

bird, and this fellow knew that he had the hunter just where he wanted him—completely in his power. What do you think that ostrich did? He dropped right down on top of the poor hunter, completely hiding him from view. That poor hunter wished he had not been so foolish as to get so near the huge bird, at least we suppose he wished so; but we shall never know just how he did feel, for when the ostrich at last arose, there lay the poor hunter just as flat as a pancake, looking very much as if he had been under a heavy rolling machine. The ostrich hurried away as fast as he could go, leaving the poor hunter to his fate. We see what a powerful bird this is and how careful the poor hunter has to be.

Vacation at Grandfather's.

VACATION had come, and Dick and I were two of the happiest boys you could find after a good long search. Vacation did not simply mean to us that examinations were over, that now books and slates could be put away, and study hour given over to play. No, indeed! Vacation

meant lots more to us, it meant Grandfather's.
If and boy has a grandfather who lives on a big
farm, with lots of horses and cows, and whose
place is just filled with trees that grow in exactly
the right style for climbing, and if he has a
grandmother who knows how to make the best
pies and puddings and ginger cake men that no
baker could possibly make half as good, then he

has some idea of what vacation meant to Dick
and me.

Grandfather's place was many miles from our
home. We had to start quite early in the morning, and ride on the train all day—then, just
about the time the sun commenced to creep down
back of the hill, the train stopped at Clearfield,
—that's the name of the station—and out we
popped, eyes wide open for the two big grays
that grandfather always drove. They never

failed us, and after getting a good big hug from grandfather, we always rubbed their soft noses, and patted their sleek, fat necks.

Grandmother knew the appetites of her two healthy grand-sons, and made ample prepara-tions. Such piles of bread and butter as she cut for us, and how good it tasted, s p r e a d with g r a n d m o t h e r's lovely b u t t e r and the golden honey that the busy bees made.

"Early to bed, and early to rise," was grand-father's motto; so we boys must wait until breakfast time to tell all the home news, and to ask after Towser, the watch-dog, and Bess, the old donkey, and to hear about the cunning gray kittens in the barn, and the little fluffy ducklings only two days old, and the baby lambs.

The sun was not up long, when grandfather called, "Dick! Rob! It's time you were a stirrin'. Don't let the outside world enjoy all the morning's loveliness; get up, and enjoy yourselves."

How we did love the well-cured ham that grandmother had for breakfast, and the new-laid eggs that were fried just right. Everything tasted wonderfully good to us boys, for hunger is a good sauce, you know.

Breakfast over, we started for the stables. It was such fun to hear the horses whinning for their share of the apples we carried to Bess, and to see the little baby colts trot coyly away as we attempted to rub their cunning faces. Our next visit was made to the calves. Nothing could be prettier than these timid little creatures. We had hard work coaxing them to be friends, but the salt held out to them was too great a temptation, and we won at last.

Aaron, the man, was milking. The milk rose in a snowy foam as it poured into the shining tin pail. We boys were great friends with Aaron, and his round red face beamed like the sun as we watched him with undisguised admiration.

"Mew! Mew!" sounded from some far away

corner. Dick went off to search for the cause, and there in an empty stall lay Malty and her four Malty babies. Aaron gave us a saucer of milk for her, and she purred gently, as though she were trying to express her thanks. The old gobbler strutted around the barnyard, seeming to suggest that he, too, was a subject for admiration.

The boy, Dan, had gone to the corn field to pull out the weeds that had gathered between the rows. Dick and I started off to join him, but what a laugh we had when we reached the top of the hill. There stood the funniest looking thing you ever saw. It was a scare-crow rigged up in an old suit of Dan's, with one of grandfather's hats on its head, a wooden gun in its hand, and a powder flask swung under its arm. But the funniest sight of all was to see a crow perched on the top of the hat, no more scared than Dick and I were.

Days went so fast that vacation was over before we realized it, and the time had come for us to go home. It was hard work to leave so much fun, but we had to make the best of it, and look forward to another summer and more happy days at Grandfather's.

Ted's Birthday Gift.

IT was Ted's birthday. Eight years ago, grandma told him as she wished him many happy returns of the day, and gave him a great, big hug and a kiss—he was just the tiniest mite of a

thing, but now she considers him quite a good size boy for his age. Ted liked to be told he was big, and he held up his head and threw back his shoulders, just to make himself as tall as ever he could.

Now papa had a birthday kiss for Ted, too,
but he had something besides that. Right alongside of Ted's chair at the table was the loveliest
red wheel-barrow, all finished off in black and

gold. You should have seen Ted's eyes when
they spied the treasure. They grew bigger and
bigger, until you might almost think they would
drop out of his head. He had wanted a wheel-
barrow for ever so long, and now that his wish
was to be fulfilled he was too pleased to say one

word.　Papa looked almost as pleased as Ted,
he did so like to make his boy happy.

Ted's birthday came in the spring. He thought
it was a beautiful time to have a birthday—the
whole outside world seemed to put on its pret-
tiest dress in honor of the day, and as Ted sat at
the table trying to eat his breakfast, but too full
of delight over his wheel-barrow to care very
much, the breezes, heavy ladened with the perfume of the blossoms, stole softly in at the half
opened windows.

Little Bess was Ted's three year old sister, and
she was also his pet and plaything. Ted was an
idol to Bess, and to share in his play was her
greatest happiness. Bess thought the new wheel-
barrow the most beautiful thing she had ever
seen.

"Go put your bonnet on, and I'll take you for
a ride," said Ted.

What fun they had, and how frightened Bess
grew when Ted trunneled her so swiftly around
the corners. Ted laughed at her fear, and went
all the faster.

But Ted's fearlessness led to sad trouble. Just
as they started at full speed down the hill, off
came the wheel, out went Bess, and the pretty

red wheel-barrow fell all to pieces. No bones
were broken, but two broken-hearted little children picked up the pieces, and went into the

house to mother. Mother kissed and petted them
both, and comforted Ted with the promise that
father would mend it and make it as good as
new.

The Little Indian Boy.

DID you ever think, when night comes and you see mother undress the baby and tuck him snugly in his snowy white bed, that perhaps there are some babies who have different cradles from his, and very different treatment, too?

The little Indian baby who lives in the north-western part of America has a very different cradle. His is only a piece of wood, sometimes birch bark, which is hollowed out. The baby is laid on the board, and his mother laces him in, passing the cord from side to side. A small piece of wood, covered with bark, is used for his pillow. When the baby's mother goes for a walk, she carries the cradle and baby on her back, the little Indian's head just peeping over his mother's shoulder. If she is busy, she hangs the cradle and baby on a tree, and the wind swings the cradle gently to and fro, often sending the little one to "Shut-eye-town." Sometimes there are tiny bells fastened to the cradle, and their tinkle, tinkle, when the wind swings it, makes very sweet music.

As soon as the little Indian boy is old enough, his father takes him with him to learn hunting and fishing. He holds the lighted torch while the old Indian spears the fish at night, and he helps him also with the canoe or boat. He soon learns to use the bow and arrow, and to bring down the birds as they fly through the air. It is the fate, at times, of some unlucky animal to stop the arrow as it comes dashing towards the ground, for of course every arrow does not pierce the object toward which it is directed.

The Indian children do not wear dainty clothes, like you little people. Sometimes they have only a piece of cloth around them serving for a skirt. The father and mother Indians wrap themselves in blankets, and the brighter the colors, the better they like them. Their hair is long and straight and black, and they love to dress it with tall, stiff feathers. Their shoes are not made like ours, but are pieces of skin, often beautifully trimmed with beads and worked with fancy silks. These shoes are called moccasins.

Once there was a little Indian boy, who lived not far from the railroad. It happened one day that the train stopped for some reason or other, and this little fellow, thinking he might coax some goodies from the passengers, sat down and cried as though his heart would break, sobbing

out from time to time how hungry he was. As
he sat there on the edge of the platform, the
people in the train felt very sorry for him, thinking he had in some way become lost, and possibly
might be starving; so, not knowing this was a
trick, pitied the poor little fellow, opened their
baskets, and generously shared their lunch with
him, giving him the very best they had. They
did not know that the father and mother were
hiding in the bushes, and that this was a scheme
of theirs to get their living. When the train
moved on, he gathered up his treasures, carried
them to his father and mother, and they had the
grandest kind of a feast. There was dainty
white bread, chicken, cakes and pies, good things
of all sorts. We should not blame the little fellow, for of course he thought it was all right, if
mother said so, just as our little boys and girls
think what their fathers and mothers say is just
right and the proper thing to do. Now this was
a very naughty trick for the little Indian boy to
play, but we must remember that he had no one
to teach him how wrong it is to deceive people,
for his father and mother had never been taught
either. It is we, who know how, who must try
to be good.

The First Pair of Trousers.

THE rain was falling thick and fast in the dim old forest. At first it had been nothing but a gentle shower, but now the great drops came dashing through the trees, twisting and turning the leaves, and even bending the swaying branches. The clouds were so thick and black that old Sol was hidden completely out of sight.

Little Cubby Bruin heard the sound of the falling rain when he opened his eyes in the hollow of the great tree in which he lived. "Oh deary, deary," muttered Cubby. "Now all my fun is spoiled. This is the day of Cousin Wolf's party, and mother will never let me go while the rain pours down in this style."

He crawled to the opening in the tree, and poked out his little head to see if there was any show of its clearing off, but the clouds hung heavy, and the rain poured down unceasingly.

Cubby crawled back again, and curled himself up for another nap. He slept once more, and dreamed of the games of catch and toss, and of the frolics of every kind that he and Cousin Wolf would enjoy together. Pretty soon he awoke to find no wolf there, and he himself tucked away in the old tree.

It was Mother Bruin that had aroused the

sleeping cub, and she was standing outside calling him a lazy fellow, and telling him to get up.

"Is it still raining, mother?" called Cubby. "Why, no," said she. "The rain has stopped, the clouds are separating to let the sun peep out, and a gentle breeze is blowing and drying the wet grass."

Cubby needed no calling now, but sprang out of the tree with a bound.

"Now, mother," said he, "I can go to Wolfy's, can't I?"

"Go to Wolfy's!" said mother. "You have nothing to wear." Cubby looked so sad that his mother felt sorry, and so she gave him a good, tight hug, and told him she would fix up something for him to wear. She went right to work, and Cubby jumped and capered around, listening to the snip, snap of her scissors as she cut and fitted her work. At last she had fashioned the cutest pair of trousers you ever saw. It was his first pair, and of course he was proud of them. He strutted around with his hands in his pockets, just as happy as he could be. This was more of a treat than Cubby had dreamed of, for he had not expected to be promoted to trousers so soon. It would be hard to tell where mother found the stuff to make them of, but they were certainly very fine. They were made of tiny red and white checked goods, and fastened over the shoulders with bright red suspenders, and the fit was exquisite.

Father and Mother Bruin were just about as proud and happy as he, and greatly pleased at their son's happiness. They could do nothing but stand and admire their boy as he stood before them in his new rig.

Cubby was so much taken up with his new clothes that he forgot all about going to Wolfy's, and it was quite late in the afternoon before he thought of it again. He did not care much, however, and told his mamma when she tucked him in bed that night that he would rather have the trousers than go to Wolfy's forty times.

The Tables Turned.

OLD JIMMY BLAKE lived in a funny sort of a shanty at the foot of a hill. He was too old to work, and he lived upon the food the neighbors gave him, and pretty good living it was, too, for the neighbors pittied old Jimmy, and many of

them remembered what good work he used to
do before the stiffness got into his old joints.

Some folks said that Jimmy lived alone, but
this was a mistake, for he shared his shanty, and
also his food, with a big, long-horned goat called
Billy. Billy loved old Jimmy dearly, and would
follow him around like a dog, but to every one
but Jimmy, Billy was the crossest goat that ever
lived. If Jimmy was out of sight, strangers
dared not venture too near the shanty.

On the top of the hill, at the bottom of which
Jimmy's shanty was built, stood the school house.
A score or more of round-faced, red-cheeked
urchins came there every day to be taught their
a-b-c's and as much other learning as their little
brains could hold, for they were so crowded with
mischief, it was hard work to wedge in any
knowledge.

Now the boys all knew old Jimmy, and they
all knew Billy, too, and Billy knew them. He
had no liking for these school children. He remembered sticks and stones that had been aimed
at him from behind trees and other hiding places.

One day the boys planned to have some fun
with Billy. One of them had seen Jimmy's
shanty tightly shut, and the goat tied to a tree.

Down the hill they started, well ladened with stones and other missiles of one sort or another, and for some time they pelted Billy to their hearts' content. But all at once the tables were turned; Billy gave one mighty leap, broke the rope, and made a dash for his tormentors. Away they flew, Billy after them as fast as he could go. It was hard work getting up the hill, but they reached the school house at last, and entered it, a lot of breathless, scared youngsters. In fact, they had never before been quite so frightened, and they all decided that, in the future, they would let Billy alone, for they might never again have such a lucky escape.

The Queen Bee's Ball.

THERE was great excitement in the meadow. As soon as dawn peeped out and said good morning to the world, and old Sol smilingly lifted his head from behind the trees in the pine woods, the fuss and confusion began. The Queen of the Bees was responsible for it all. She had decided to give a ball, and had bidden her mes-

sengers fly far and near to tell all the insects in
the meadow to come and join in the jolly dance
that night.   One flew here, and another flew

there, their
noisy buzz, buzz,
as they flew
from place to
place making a
constant din.

A merry band
of fiddlers lived
in the swamp,
and the Queen's
favorite messen-
ger had been dispatched there in great haste, for
you see, they were needed to provide the music
for the dancing.

The katy-dids in their pretty green gowns
were invited to sing a duet, half singing "Katy-
did," and half responding with "Katy-didn't."
The Queen Bee liked the crickets, and so did all
the bees; they were such cheerful little fellows,
and so, of course, they were invited, and they
one and all accepted the invitation, for crickets
never miss a chance for having fun, especially
when katy-dids are around.

The spider, who was weaving a web in the
spruce tree, sent his
compliments to her royal
highness, the Queen,
and bade the messenger
tell her it would be his
pleasure to come, but it
was impossible for him
to leave his beautiful
web, that was so nearly
finished. This message
did not please Madame
Queen very well, for
she was always happiest when having her own
way.

The locusts had just shed their shells, and
were attired in their new spring suits, so they
accepted the invitation gladly, for the vain little
fellows thought it would be great fun to show
their fine clothes, even if they were not so giddy
as the yellow jackets, whose striped coat was the
envy of all the insects.

Tiny Mrs. Lady-bug promised to come, if she
could find any one to stay with her babies, for
only the night before she had left them alone,
and she had been so nervous she had had no

pleasure, for
she kept
hearing all
the time,
"Lady-bug,
lady-bird, fly
away home;
your house
is on fire,
your children

will burn." So she had made up her mind that
she would not leave them alone again.

Grand-daddy-long-legs thought he had grown
too old for balls, but the messengers coaxed so
hard that he promised to take a good long nap,
and to honor the occasion with his presence.

The sun was shining in all his glory, and the
hour of noon had arrived before all the guests
had been notified. The messengers were weary
from their busy morning, and hid themselves in
the hearts of the flowers or among the tall, graceful grasses to fall asleep, and so refresh themselves that they, too, might be ready for the fun
and frolic the evening was to bring.

We could not begin to tell all the pleasant
things that happened, but one was the meeting
of Yellow-jacket and Miss Gauzy Wings. They

had not been friends for a long time, but they met this day on their way to the ball, and found each other's company so pleasant that ere long

Yellow-jacket was on his knees, suing for Miss Gauzy Wing's hand in marriage, and he must have been accepted, for he was very attentive to

her all through the evening, and when the ball
was over, and all the insects said good-night and
hastened away to their
homes, they departed
hand in hand, and be-
fore very long there
was a gathering of the
insects to celebrate the
wedding of this happy pair.   So the Queen Bee's
Ball was the means of bringing about the event.

Widow Murphy's Pig.

EVERYBODY knew her—she sold apples at the
crossing, and her cheeks were as red and her
smile as sweet as the tempting fruit that made
the children's eyes sparkle with delight.   Rain
or shine, she sat there, her stiff green bonnet
crowning her head in summer, and her big black
bonnet almost hiding her cherry face in winter.

The great gingham umbrella that shielded her
from rain and sun was often also the sheltering
place of many an unlucky school boy caught in
a shower.

She lived on a tiny place, just outside the

town, and when Jack, the lame newsboy, or Ted, the black boot-black, or when any of her regular customers stopped for a chat, she loved to tell them of her "foine pratie patch that did so well, thanks to her airly risin," and of the hens that troubled her so by scratching in this much-prized garden, in spite of all the corn she scattered for their comfort.

But by and by she revelled in a new treasure —a cunning black pig. One day, when Widow Murphy went to the farm house for her daily can of milk—the farmer's wife gave it to her, and what a prize it was to the poor old soul. 'Twas sick and tiny and forlorn looking enough when she got it, but she nursed it most carefully, and its queer little grunt was like music to her ears. Piggy learned to know her, and followed her around like a dog, and he really grew fatter every day in his comfortable new home.

One morning, it was time to go to town with apples—and time for Piggy to be shut in his pen; he was far too precious to be left roaming around—but where was he? The widow searched everywhere, and called and called, until at last she gave up in despair, and tired out, sat down upon the well curb to rest and think.

Then she heard a noise that made her jump up in such a hurry that the ruffles on her snowy cap almost danced. It was piggy's grunt, and it certainly came from the well. Way over leaned the old lady—and scarcely could she believe her own eyes, for there in the bucket, safe and sound, sat that naughty black pig. He had been peering over the well, perhaps, admiring his funny snout in the clear waters below, lost his balance, and tumbled in, fortunately into the bucket that hung down low.

How glad the widow was to find him, and how the boys laughed when she told them the tale. We hope that piggy learned a lesson, and became ever after a less vain and less curious piggy.

But one day a man came from a distant city to buy a fine little pig for a Thanksgiving feast. Widow Murphy did not want to sell, but the price offered was too tempting, so she finally agreed to sell him. If she could have looked into that house on Thanksgiving Day, she would have seen piggy perched on a big platter in the center of the table.

A Chance Acquaintance.

Miss Rhody Run had grown tired of her home in the stable loft. It used to be very nice when the boys used to play there, because they were sure to drop crumbs of the cakes and crackers they were forever eating. But now the boys had gone away to school, and Rhody felt very lonely. Of course she had plenty to eat, for it was not much trouble to find her way to the feed box, and John, the coachman, was not always careful to drop the lid; but Rhody thought there was something in this world to think about besides eating. She missed the merry laugh and the happy voices of the children, and she grew more lonely every day. She finally made up her mind that she would leave her home in the stable, and travel around the country until she found a place where she could be happy. Early one morning she started off, her red flannel cape pinned around her shoulders, and an old salt bag, in which she carried all her treasures, slung over her shoulder. The village was just waking as she trotted through the streets. The shop-keepers were just taking down their shutters and opening their doors, and as this was all new to Rhody, she thought she would step inside, and see what was going on. She wanted to do this very badly, but she could not get courage.

As the day grew older, and the noise and con-

fusion increased, she was so frightened that she hid herself under a molasses barrel that was propped up on the sidewalk. After things began to grow quiet again, she dared to venture out and continue her journey. She was getting pretty hungry by this time, so she timidly crept into a bakery, and succeeded in getting a good meal, for the baker was not the tidiest man in the world, and there were plenty of crumbs on the floor.

The next day found Rhody wandering along the river bank, where the pond lilies grew and the tall brown cat-tails nodded in the wind. All at once Rhody was startled by the sound of a strange voice, and turning, saw a spry young frog at her side. "I see," said he, "that you are admiring our river and its pretty, flowery banks. Let me walk along with you, and enjoy it also, for though it is not new to me, it is ever beautiful."

"What a very nice creature this is," thought Rhody; so she dropped him a courtesy, and told him she was very glad of his company, and Froggy, pleased with her approval of him, did his level best to be entertaining. Rhody was charmed with her companion, and the two chatted as if they had long been friends. Froggy was very much interested in Rhody's story about her home in the stable and her trips to the feed box for food, and very much surprised to learn that she had never before seen the river. So he told all about the wonderful times he had in his watery home, and she was greatly interested in all he had to relate. She said it might be very pleasant, but she did not think she would like

it, although some of her cousins lived in the water a great deal of the time.

"How sorry I am," said Froggy, "that I cannot ask you to dine with me; but my larder contains no such food as you would eat; worms and flies and tiny fish are not to your liking, I am sure, and then I have to take a sail on the river in order to reach my home, and that would not please you either. I am sorry that we cannot enjoy each other's society longer, but, as it is now lunch time, I shall have to say good-bye."

So, after best wishes on both sides that they might some day meet again, Froggy boarded a floating leaf, and went sailing down the stream to his home, while Rhody continued on her journey alone. She felt more lonesome than ever after Froggy had left her, and she almost wished she had not met him at all, since he could not go with her all the way. She was almost tempted to go back and wait until he came ashore again, but she finally decided to keep on her journey, hoping that chance might again bring her a friend that would be as charming as Sir Froggy.

The Foxes' Quarrel.

FALL had come with its brown, withered grasses and fallen leaves. Of late Jack Frost had been blowing his keen breath over hill and dale, turning the leaves to crimson and gold, and opening the chestnut burrs, so that the ripe nuts might fall to the earth. One night, when the moon had hidden its face behind a cloud, Darius Sharp and Christopher Sly, two youthful foxes, set out to find some game. Farmer Tobbin lived not far from the foxes' home, and this man's good wife, Dame Tobbin, was noted far and near for her beautiful poultry. Now this bit of ews had reached the ears of Darius and Christopher, and was greeted by them with great joy. Maybe you have guessed that these young creatures had planned to try for game at the farmer's. Well, you are right. Only this very morning they had planned to go as soon as it was night, if the moon did not shine too brightly. Fortune seemed to favor them, and at the appointed hour they met, and proceeded towards the farm house. Darius took his brother Xerxes along to help bring home the game, if they should be fortunate enough to secure more than

they could carry themselves. As they hurried
along, they met many of their friends going out
on hunting expeditions, for the night was favor-
able. Presently they reached the home of
Farmer Tobbin, and quietly and carefully entered the yard, knowing that the slightest noise
would be sure to waken Bruno, the faithful
watch-dog, and set the cocks crowing, and then
it would be all over with them, for the farmer
would appear with his gun. As they entered
the yard, they caught sight of a rooster which
had sauntered out to see if it were yet dawn.
Quick as a wink, Darius seized him, while
Christopher secured a plump, fat duck that had
forgotten to go inside to roost. In the excitement, poor little Xerxes was quite forgotten,
and the friends, throwing their game across their
shoulders, started for home, well pleased with
their luck. Just as they entered the woods, a
snipe met the eyes of Christopher, but before
he had captured it, Darius caught sight of it.
Both rushed for it, and seized it. Now, whose
should it be? Both claimed it. Long and
angrily the foxes quarreled. Christopher claimed
it because he saw it first, and Darius claimed it
because he got hold of it first. Morning came

and they were still disputing. Suddenly Bruno, the dog, appeared on the scene, and they both scampered off as fast as they could go, leaving snipe, duck and chicken behind. Bruno had a kingly breakfast, while the silly foxes had none. When they got back to their homes, and sat down to think over the matter, they were sorry enough to think they had been so greedy, for in trying to get all, each one had lost the little he had. Poor little Xerxes had been forgotten in their hurry to get away with their prizes.

New Year's Eve.

THE snow lay deep upon the ground and nestled among the leafless branches of the forest trees, gleaming and sparkling like millions of diamonds. There was no sign of its melting, for the days were bitter cold, and the nights even colder, if anything.

"It is the coldest winter for many years," said old Daddy Bruin, and he ought to know, for he had lived longer in the forest than the rest of the animals.

Daddy Bruin and his old wife had built a house with the branches of trees closely packed together, and had covered the roof with thick coatings of mud. There they lived, as snug and comfortable as you please. The wind whistled all around them, but it could not enter their dwelling and bother them, so snugly were they housed.

It was New Year's Eve in the forest, and Daddy Bruin had invited all the inhabitants thereof to meet with him in his home to talk about the past year. Beasts of every shape, size and color gathered at his call, and even the wise old owl, having heard of the gathering, came with his little son. When they had all arrived, Daddy wrapped himself in his blanket, and put on his Tam O'Shanter, and seating himself on a fallen log, began to talk to the eager group in his usual kind fashion. They all looked very much interested, and paid the best of attention to Bruin's remarks, even to the tiny little mice that sat close by his feet. I suppose you would like to know what they were talking about, so I will tell you. Bruin was trying to get them to give up their bad habits and live good lives. He said he had decided not to steal anything more

from the farmers, but would hereafter depend
on the fruits of field and wood for his living.

One after another the animals confessed that
they had done lots of bad things during the year,

for which they were sorry. Even Winky Blinky, the owl, looked very grave as he sat listening to these tales and confessions of evil doing. The subject was so interesting that they talked together for hours, even far into the night.

It was a very solemn meeting, and brought good results, for

"There, beneath the swaying trees,
　As round them played the whistling breeze,
　And from the sky, the queen of night
　Looked down upon the pleasing sight,
　With many a vow and promise true,
　They all resolved to start anew;

'And, let us hope, in after days
They followed peaceful, honest ways;

That guns and snares and traps severe
,Were not required throughout the year."

Bomba, the Merry Old King.

THERE is an island to the south of Italy, called Sicily. The weather is beautiful there, and flowers and fruits grow most plentifully. Here, so the story goes, lived a king, called Bomba. Bomba was known as the merry old King, for he loved to play and romp and frolic, notwithstanding the fact that his hair had grown white as the driven snow, and his beard had also been touched by time's frosty hand.

He lived in the royal palace with no one but his servants, more than a dozen of whom were kept to amuse and entertain this fun-loving sovereign. The grounds around the court were all devoted to his pleasures. There he played tennis, or enjoyed a game of ball, or else rigged himself in his suit, and became one of the players in a jolly game of foot-ball. If Bomba did not feel like taking part in the game, he would order his servants to play in their very best style; perhaps he would be umpire, or perhaps he would make himself comfortable, and devote his time to enjoying the fun.

Bomba loved to roll a hoop. His was made of the most beautiful red gold, and the stick he

used for rolling it was nothing less than his own
jeweled sceptre.   It was the funniest sight to see
Bomba dashing after the hoop, his crown, pulled
tightly down on his head, gleaming in the sunlight, and his purple gown, richly trimmed with
ermine, flying about him in all directions.   The
marbles he used were made of gold, and his tops
were of gold, too, set with precious stones of
every kind and color.   How they sparkled and
gleamed as the top went spinning around and
around, and how old Bomba clapped his hands
and roared with delight.

Now people thought, and they dared do no
more than think, that their king was crazy. You
see, if this had reached Bomba's ears, there is no
telling what might have happened to the person
who said it.   But still, the people had their own
thoughts, and they felt very sad to think their
king was really nothing but a foolish, fun-loving
child.   They wished some one, wise and good,
might wear the purple robe, and the jeweled
crown, and use the royal sceptre for some better
purpose than rolling a golden hoop.

One morning, after Bomba had eaten his
breakfast, and a good meal it was too, he called
his jester to him.   He told him to summon his

entertainers, bid them dress in their merriest
costumes, and hasten to the great court garden.
The jester went to do his bidding, and one and
all wondered what scheme old Bomba now had.
They were all present when the king came
among them. He gazed at them, laughed merrily at their rigs, and told them that now he was
ready for a game of leap-frog; they should take
turns at being the frog, while he did the leaping.
This soon became a favorite sport with the king,
and every day he would spend a portion of the
time in this kind of play. People from all
around came to see this merry old king indulge
in the games and sports which children love.
But, alas! for the king; he tried the game once
too often. One day, when he had been having
a particularly jolly game, and been more reckless
than was his want, he tried to jump over one of
his servants, who was very tall, but he missed
his leap, slipped and fell, and lay a helpless
heap, never to rise again. The courtiers gathered around him, trying to do something for
him, for at first they thought he was only
stunned, but all the doctors could do nothing,
and at last they realized that their king was indeed dead. It was a sad death for the merry

old monarch, and all the people pitied him, even though he had been nothing but a foolish old king, and they missed his merry laugh and his kind, gentle face. They missed him more and more as the days went by, and there was no fun in the palace. The next king was a very stern, hard master, and they often wished they were again living under merry old King Bomba, though he did spend most of his time in idle sport.

A Friendly Pair.

WINTER had given way to spring, and the alligator had come out of the hole in the banks of the river in which he had slept away the chilly nights and days. He felt so strong and happy after his long sleep, and having given himself a vigorous shake and oft repeated stretches, he dived into the water for a cool, refreshing bath. This done, his thoughts turned toward something to eat, and he opened and shut his big jaws, as if smacking his lips, when he thought of the delightful prospect, and there arose before him visions of the shiny-backed fish that he would catch and dine upon.

In a tiny stream that flowed through the
marshes lived a fish that could be found no-

where else. Mr. Alligator liked this fish so well
that he decided to go fishing in the stream, and

if possible bring back a few of these fine fat fellows for his dinner. So he slung his bag over his shoulder, and taking his good stout walking stick, he started off on his tramp.

A shaggy brown bear, who lived in the woods, had just come out of the great hollow tree where he had found a resting place during the winter months. His store of provisions was exhausted, and he thought it high time to start out in search of more. He blinked and winked at the bright sunshine, and he smiled and nodded at the little flowers that seemed to greet him in their own pretty way. But the feeling of hunger was stronger than the attractions of nature, and so Mr. Bear donned his beaver hat, and taking his market bag on his arm, he too started out to get something to eat. He thought he might be able to find a pile of nuts in some bushes near the river, for he remembered having left some there in the fall.

Now it happened that the stream where the fish lived, and the bushes where the nuts were hidden, were close together, so it was not strange that the bear and the alligator should come across each other. "Good morning," said the alligator, "are you off on a journey?" "Not far," said the bear, "I am only taking a morning walk in search of something to eat." "Well, I am on the same errand," said the alligator; "if our ways are together, shall we not walk together?" This plan suited the bear, so they walked together side by side, and enjoyed a pleasant stroll.

The Balky Mule Outwitted.

AMONG a forest of cypress, fir and pine trees stood the palace of old Sultan Allah Baba, with its cupolas and domes towering high above the wilderness of trees. It was built of white marble, and kept always, at the order of the Sultan, gleamingly white and beautiful. The windows were of the most gorgeous colors, through which the sun brightly shone, sending rainbow-like shadows in and around the rooms of the palace. At night the place was lighted by jeweled, studded lamps, which were hung from the ceilings by great silken cords.

Allah Baba had once been a tall, stately young fellow, but the happy, easy life he had led, together with the many dainties that daily filled his table, had added many pounds to the Sultan's weight. He liked this change in his appearance as little as he did the snow white beard that had taken the place of the jet black whiskers.

The great cap that adorned his head covered the growth of snowy hair, but no such device hid the whiskers from sight.

"I am growing old," mused the Sultan, "and that will never do. I must find some plan to bring me back my youth again. I'll dye my whiskers, but how can I rid myself of all this load of flesh?"

Allah Baba thought and thought, but all in vain. Finally he sent for one of the wise men of his court, and stating the case to him, asked what he should do.

"Your case is easily settled, your Highness," said he. "I am sure you would soon be as slender as a young willow if you would only ride a mule."

"A delightful plan that," said the Sultan. "I will reward you richly for your noble efforts."

No time was lost in buying the mule, and of course they tried to select the very best in all the land. The Sultan came from the palace to examine the new treasure, and smiled approvingly at the animal's long ears and shaggy coat.

"Now I'll mount him," said Allah Baba, "and go dashing away on my first ride."

It was easy enough to mount, but the dashing away did not follow. Not one inch would the mule move. Allah Baba coaxed and pulled, but for nought; his mule would not stir.

"Cut me a stick," roared Allah; "I'll teach him a lesson or two." But the stick, likewise, proved useless. At last Allah grew desperate.

"A fortune," said he, "to the man who makes this miserable beast move!"

"I'll earn it in no time, your Highness," said one of his servants. Right to work he went, and after several hours' labor he rigged the troublesome mule in a complete set of sails. Then, again, Allah mounted his steed, and away they went, this time without the least trouble, for old longears had to go, whether he would or not. The wind filled the sails, and the mule was surprised at himself to think he could go so fast. As they sped along over the road, everything and everybody fled before them, for they knew not what to make of the queer looking object. It was a lively ride for the old Sultan, but what pleased him best of all, was the conquering of the balky mule, and he was really conquered, too. For several days the old Sultan took his daily ride on his sail-rigged beast, but one day he decided to try him without all these things, so he told his servants to bring him to the door with nothing but a saddle and bridle on. They obeyed, but were quite sure that when their master attempted to make the mule go, he would again show his ugly temper. Great was their surprise, therefore, to see him start off at just as rapid a rate as ever, as soon as their master mounted his back, showing that he had discovered that the Sultan was master of the situation. He never again was obliged to use the device which had been so useful to him, but always found his mule ready to obey his slightest word.

Fun in the Woods.

REX WOLF and his friend, Teddy Fox, had played catch with the fallen blossoms until they were weary; then they played a game of hokey, but found it no fun. After this they tried hide and go seek and leap-frog, but nothing seemed to please them. So they had seated themselves

on the soft green grass, and both their little
heads were busy trying to think what next to
do. To be quiet was out of the question, and
no nice kind of fun seemed to suggest itself.

Foxy suddenly clapped his hands with glee.

"I have it, Rex," said he. "Do you remember
the great oak log that the woodcutters left here
last week? We will put a board across, and
have as fine a see-saw as you or I could want."

"Good for you, Teddy," said his friend. "I

knew you would think of something before
long."

Off these two youngsters scampered, and having found a fallen limb near at hand, they soon
had it placed across the stump, and were taking
a fine ride. Up and down they went, thoroughly
enjoying this new kind of sport.

Just about this time, a fat, black bear came
strolling along.

"Give me a ride, Foxy?" said he.

"Yes, if you like," said Foxy. "Rex and I
will get on one side, and you can get on the
other."

Pretty soon they were all ready to start again.
Rex and Teddy got on one end, and away they
went up in the air, just as soon as the old black
bear took his seat on the other, and there they
stayed, too, for the old bear was so heavy that
they could not lift him up. "This won't do,"
said Teddy. "You are too heavy for us." So
he called to a little porcupine, who was watching the fun. "Get on," Prickly, and help us
balance old Fatty." So Prickly crawled up, and
they just balanced the old fellow. Then they
had the greatest fun; now up, now down, until
at last they got dizzy and tired, too. Then they

thought they would play a trick on the old bear,
so the three little fellows all jumped off together, letting old Fatty down rather suddenly.
But he was such a good-natured fellow that he
did not mind it, and invited them to go home

with him, and they joyfully accepted the invitation.

Now Blacky's sister had at one time found an
accordion that some people had left in the woods,
and she kept it hidden in the old hollow oak
where she lived. Blacky had told his friends of
this treasure, so when they had chatted awhile,

Teddy Fox begged Miss Blacky to play for them.
She willingly consented, and seating herself
upon a log, began to play with all her might.
It was not long before quite a merry party had
gathered on the green, and among them were
two bright little hares. They began to dance a
jig to the lively music that was being played,
and soon others joined them, and soon all were
enjoying a good jolly dance.

Just before the party broke up, and they went
away, the bear proposed that they should sit
down and chat awhile. Then he suggested that
they should form a sort of a club, and have a
meeting every week in the old woods. He said
his sister would learn how to play some new
pieces, especially dance music, and he thought
they could have a fine time together. This they
all thought would be great fun, and so they decided to meet each Tuesday at five o'clock for
a good old frolic.

The Monks' Victory.

THE pale moon never shed her light nor the
stars never twinkled over a more sorrowful spot

than the little village of Thimble Top. Everything was once so bright and happy, and care
and trouble were strangers, but now they had
come among the villagers as most unwelcome
guests, and there they seemed to mean to
stay.

The trouble was caused by Diddle Dee, a
wicked, merciless tyrant, who captured little
children, and put them to cruel tortures. He
lived in a mighty castle, so strongly barred and
bolted that no one could enter. There was
scarcely a house in the village but had suffered
from the ravages of this dreadful Diddle Dee.
Mothers, who thought they watched their little
ones most carefully, turned their backs but for
an instant, and the child was gone—and not a
trace could be found of the thief or the captive.
How he bore the child off to his castle without
being seen by a soul, was a mystery no one
could solve. Matters kept growing worse and
worse, and no help could be found.

But one day two pious monks visited the village on a pilgrimage. As they rode through the
streets, news of the sad goings on reached their
ears and filled their hearts with deep sorrow.
They were wise, as they were good, and they

went straight to work to find some way out of the difficulty.

"We will go boldly to Diddle Dee," said one of the monks, "and see if our sacred calling will not have some weight with him."

Now it happened that Diddle Dee dreaded nothing so much as the ill will of these holy men, so when they rode up to the castle, he received them very graciously. The two monks dismounted, tied their beasts to a couple of trees, and entered the house of Diddle Dee. In the room into which he led them burned a bright fire, and over the fire swung an enormous kettle filled with water.

"A boiling pot for the helpless little ones," thought one of the fathers, "but it has served its day for that use—only one more victim shall ever fill it, and that is Diddle Dee himself." With that he laid hold of the wicked fellow, and with the aid of his brother monk, plunged him into the pot.

The water was hot, and Diddle Dee screamed for mercy, but the monks paid no heed to him until he was scared almost to death.

"Now," said the monk who had seized him, "are you willing to promise to leave this country

and your wicked work forever? We will take
you to a place where you can do much good,
and perhaps blot out some of your wicked past."

Diddle Dee was only too glad to promise anything, and when he was lifted out of the pot,
stood before the fathers a humbled and sadder
man.

The monks tied Diddle Dee to his own iron
bed, for they had no wish to lose their prize.
Then they looked around to see what they could
find. Quantities of good things filled the larder,
and they soon had the air heavy with the delicious odor of cooking food. When all was
finished, one of the monks rode to the village to
tell the anxious villagers of their victory, and to
bid them celebrate the event with them in feasting. The feast which the monks had prepared
was truly wonderful and surpassed anything that
had ever been held in the village before. It
was indeed an occasion for great joy, since now
the village was free from the ravages of this
terrible creature, whose evil deeds had made life
almost a burden, especially to those who had
little ones in their families; therefore it is not
surprising that the monks found people so ready
to accept their invitations. Everybody came,

old and young, and the place was crowded. Speeches were made, thanks were offered, and cheer after cheer went up for the brave, good monks. Happiness once more reigned in the village, and Diddle Dee found that good deeds brought more satisfaction than cruelties. This was a great victory, and the people never forgot the kindness of the monks.

The Brownies' Kind Deed.

LITTLE PETER, one of the Brownies, had perched himself on the trunk of a fallen tree to think. His tiny, round face did not wear its usual smile, and his bright, black eyes had a worried look. Young Toby Tumble, passing through the woods, saw

his little friend, Peter, and scrambled up alongside of him. "You look blue, little Peter," said he, "have things gone wrong with you? Tell me what the matter is, and maybe I can help you."

"You are very kind," said little Peter, "but it is not about myself I feel so grieved, but about the Widow Good and her two little children. To-morrow is Christmas, you know, and I heard her say that she had nothing for them, so there is no prospect of a good time at the Good cottage."

Toby Tumble was looking grave himself by this time, and he sat with his face buried in his tiny hands. "I have it," said he, "they'll do it, I'm sure," and he clapped his hands in glee. "Do what?" said Peter. "Help us, to be sure. We will call all the Brownies together, tell them all about the matter, and I am sure that neither Widow Good or her little ones will want for anything to make up a Christmas dinner."

No time was to be lost in carrying out their plans, and so they hastened out to find their comrades. Of course the good Brownies were all glad to help them, for they delight to help good people.

Their first movement was to borrow a large basket from Greengoods, the grocer. The Brownies had no money, so they decided to fill the basket from the shop, and pay the master in work, for Brownies, you know, are very clever creatures, and can turn a hand at anything. The

little fellows could scarcely move the basket when filled, but all worked together, and by and by they had it mounted on sticks, and then, five or six on a side, they bore it along very comfortably.

How proud they felt as they looked at this well-filled basket! As they went along, they could see peeping from the covering of the basket, links of sausage, a fish, and the black feet of the big turkey that was to be such a treat to the children on the morrow.

They were very tired when they reached the widow's house, so they sat down to rest until morning. When light came, and all the busy little fellows had hidden themselves where they could see and not be seen, Toby Tumble knocked at the door. He had only just time to run out of sight himself, when the widow opened it. The Brownies had worked hard, but they felt fully rewarded when they saw the joy and happiness on the poor woman's face, and they decided that they would remember her again the next year, and that they would fully repay the grocer for all his goods, and would do it so quickly and thoroughly that he would never miss them.

You may be sure the widow was very happy.

when she unpacked that basket, and found all the good things, for she felt that now she could give her children a little pleasure on Christmas day. She could not imagine who it could be that had remembered her and her little ones, but her little son Rob said he was sure it was the Brownies.

A Pair of Pets.

BROWN PEGGY, the horse, did not like the strange yelping and squealing that disturbed her rest. It seemed to come from right beneath the feed box, and she feared to move, lest she should tread on the cause of all the noise, for she knew by the sound that it was alive. The stable was too dark to see, and she had to wait until Michael came and threw open the great doors. Then Peggy stepped back in her stall, and looking down, she saw, huddled close together, four of the cutest little brown puppies you ever saw. They twisted around and around, and rolled over each other in the most restless manner.

When Michael came with Peggy's breakfast, he too heard the queer noise, and looking over the feed box, he spied the little strangers. "Well, if you are not about as cute and cunning as anything I ever saw," said he. "I shall keep one of you little chaps, and I think it will be you, old fellow, for I like your snowy nose." So spoke Michael, as he leaned over and picked up one of the tiny puppies, the tip of whose nose was snowy white.

Michael had some little brothers and sisters at home, and so one day, when the puppies were old enough to leave their mother, and he was ready for his homeward walk, he remembered the little white nosed pup, and thought how much the children would enjoy playing with it, so puppy was tucked away in Michael's pocket and taken to his new quarters, where his happy new life began. The children were delighted with their new playmate, and did all in their power to make him welcome.

They had another pet, that had held full sway before the puppy came, and that was a little red pig. He was always a very tiny pig, and had grown so little that he still looked like a baby pig, although many months had gone by since his entrance into the world.

Piggy did not like the idea of a rival, and

behaved very cross and ugly, but the children scolded him, and talked to him, and by and by, when he had gotten over his pouting, he visited the little dog, and before very long they were the best friends in the world.

Jack, the Giant of the Sea.

MANY, many years ago there lived a great and powerful giant, whose name was Jack. He was as tall as some of the houses in the village where he made his home, and so strong and powerful that the earth trembled when he walked. His cane was the trunk of a tree which he had torn up by the roots and stripped of its branches. Do you wonder the people trembled with fear even at his name? His home was not built of wood or bricks, like ours. He lived in a cave down by the sea, and against this cave the waves beat day and night. Old Jack loved to hear them surge against his rocky home, and he would chuckle with delight when a heavy storm sent the breakers dashing over his cave. "Ha, ha!" roared he, "more fun for old Jack. The fishermen will

think that the fury of the waves carried off their
nets, but this old chap knows better; he knows

who stole their nets full of fish and carried them
home on his back. It was old Jack. Ha, ha, ha!"

By and by this old giant grew so wicked that he would watch from the door of his cave until he saw the fishing boats near the shore. Then into the water he would plunge, and boldly grab a net filled with the labor of a long, hard night, throw it over his back, and bear it to his cave, and the poor fishermen could do nothing but work bravely to save their own lives.

The fishermen suffered from the bold, bad deeds of this wicked Jack, but they were not the only ones. "Fish is good food," said Jack, "but sometimes I relish a good fat ox." Then it was that he would leave his cave, and with his long, powerful strides hasten to the fields where the cattle were grazing. It took him no time to throw an ox over his shoulder and bear it away to his cave. When he wanted a change, he would pick up a sheep and bear it home in one hand. One day Jack made up his mind to go fishing. "A fine fish I'll have for my supper," said he. A tall sappling served him for a pole, and a rope that had been tied to a cow he had stolen the night before answered for a line, and he made his hook from a huge bolt, bending it into shape with his strong fingers. He soon pulled in a large salmon, and threw out his line

for another trial.   Presently he felt something
pull on the line.   He had never before felt such

a tug, and he felt that whatever there was at the
other end of the line, it was pulling him more

strongly than he could pull it. Before he could
save himself, a huge sea monster rose above the

surface of the water, and jerked him from the rock, and drew him out faster and faster into the sea. The people of the village rushed to the shore, and cheered long and loud when they saw Jack in such a sorry plight. They never saw him again, for the waves and the monster bore him away farther and still farther, until at last he was lost to sight. If he did not drown, we hope he learned to be a better giant.

A Thanksgiving Tale.

OLD UNCLE NATHAN HOWE and his wife Debby lived in a tiny farm house, painted white. The shutters were green, and in summer a rose climbed up the sides of the house, almost covering this little dwelling place with its leaves and dark red roses. People driving by leaned from their carriages to take a peep at Uncle Nathan's cottage, and they smiled, as though pleased with the sight that had rewarded their efforts.

But now the bloom had left the rose, and the leaves had fallen one by one, until only a few yellow stragglers lingered.

Uncle Nathan and Aunt Debby, as everybody called them, lived all alone in their tiny white house, for they had neither kith nor kin to share it with them. Thanksgiving Day was drawing near, and Aunt Debby was busy making pumpkin pies, and plum pudding, frying doughnuts, and revelling in cooking to her heart's content. "Such a pile of stuff," thought she, "for two old people to get rid of. Of course I shall send some to the minister, and some to Dr. Brown, but then there will be enough left to feed a big family." And this last idea set Aunt Debby to thinking harder than ever.

When Uncle Nathan came in to his dinner, he found his good wife with a very thoughtful face.

"How does the poultry look, Nathan?" said she. Uncle Nathan smiled at the question, for the poultry fell to his care, and Aunt Debby never bothered about it.

"What is in the air now, old wife?" said he, somewhat surprised.

"Answer my question, and I'll tell you," she replied.

Now was Uncle Nathan's turn to look grave. "They are lookin' poorly, Debby," said he, "poorer than I ever saw 'em lookin' afore. But there is a prime young gobbler and a duck or two, as pretty as you'd want to see."

Now I'll tell you a secret. These wise fowls had determined not to be the victims of Uncle Nathan's axe, and furnish somebody's Thanksgiving dinner, so they had gone without the food Uncle Nathan scattered for them for so long that now they were the weakest, sickest, most miserable looking things you could imagine. But there was a wilful young turkey and a pair of silly ducks, who said they had no fear of the axe, and could keep away from it.

"That's plenty," said Aunt Debby, when she had heard of the gobbler and two ducks. "Now I'll tell you my plans. I've cooked more than enough for us two, Nathan, and I want to ask the Widow Love and her six children here to Thanksgiving dinner. The dinner will do them all good, and I calculate we will get enough happiness out of it to last us a week.

"And my three best fowls are for poor Widow Love and her six youngsters, hey? Well, I call that a pretty good disposal to make of them, old wife, and I guess if you can make enough pies and puddings and cakes to fill 'em up, I

can do my part with the poultry and garden
stuff."

And so the thing was settled, and when milking was done that night, Uncle Nathan and Aunt
Debby stepped across to the widow's, to ask if
they were willing to come. To be sure they
were, and there never was a more joyful Thanksgiving than this. They all ate till they could
hardly move, and went home tired and sleepy,
but very happy.

Fiddle-Cum-Fee.

A LONG, long time ago there was a little village called Harmony. It lay between two tall
mountains that sheltered it from the storms and
tempests that swept over the neighboring towns.
A beautiful stream flowed into the valley below,
watering the earth and causing it to be very
fertile. The grass grew very green and beautiful
in this tiny village, and the fruit and flowers
were larger and more abundant than anywhere
around. The people loved their homes, and
spared no pains or time in making them as beautiful as they possibly could.

But one day sorrow came to the village. Old
Fiddle-Cum-Fee had heard of the beauties of
the village of Harmony, and had left his home
some hundred miles away to visit this much-

talked-of place. Fiddle-Cum-Fee was a great
and powerful giant, feared and dreaded by all
who heard of him. He started off one morning
bright and early, so as to reach the village while

the day was yet young, and he could do this easily, for he wore shoes that carried him many miles at a single stride. Most of the villagers were seated at their tables, quietly enjoying their morning meal, when, all of a sudden, the tables commenced to rock, plates jumped up and down, cups danced in the saucers, and even the houses seemed to tremble and shake. The people looked at each other in silence, feeling sure that an earth-quake had come to destroy their little village, and perhaps bring death to many of them. Then they all rushed to their doors, and looked out, and then hastened out of doors, and were terrified to see the terrible giant coming through the street. It was his great weight that was shaking the village, and his mighty laugh, when he saw the fear and wonder of the people, sounded like a great clap of thunder. "Good people," said he, as he halted in the center of the town, "I am Fiddle-Cum-Fee; use me well, and I will be your friend, but use me badly, and you will see how Fiddle-Cum-Fee can repay your bad treatment. I am tired of my mountain home, and need a change. Your village seems to suit my purpose, so I am come to dwell among you until such time as it seems best to me to go away. I have had nothing to eat as yet this morning, so bring on your very best meat, your whitest bread, your choicest fowl and finest fruit, and I will give you a show of a fine healthy appetite. If some one will play sweet music, the time will pass more pleasantly." Almost paralyzed with fear, the people hurried away to do his bidding, while Fiddle-Cum-Fee seated himself under an apple tree, for no house could possibly hold him. It seemed as though the terrible monster would never get enough, and all were kept busy satisfying his demands. Breakfast over, Fiddle-Cum-Fee wandered back to the mountain side to take a nap, for he felt smothered in the little village. When he was gone, the people put their heads together, and tried to think of some way in which they could get rid of him, for they knew that they could never supply his wants. Plan after plan was suggested and discussed, and at last they decided to cook him a great kettle full of soup. Their idea was to prepare a fine lot of soup, place in it a drug, the fumes of which would overpower him as he leaned over to eat. When he became drowsy, they intended to pitch him over into the soup, and scald him to death. Then they would put

him on a raft, and set him adrift on the stream,
letting the current bear him off to sea. Some
of the kinder-hearted people could not bear to
do this cruel act, even to so great an enemy, and

so they finally persuaded the rest to rig up a
monstrous balloon, and when he was drowsy
from the effects of the drug, they fastened him
in a basket and sent him up. Higher and higher
the balloon rose, until, finally, it was lost to

sight. Then suddenly they saw it appear again, and they saw it coming nearer and nearer to the earth. They were greatly frightened for fear it would drop on the land, but a favoring breeze bore it out to sea, and presently it sunk, never to be seen again.

The Back Yard Party.

Mrs. Mouse laid down her pen and breathed a sigh of relief. She had been busily at work getting out invitations for a grand garden party in the back yard, and now she had finished. The field mice, the mice at the barn and wagon house, and of course the house mice, all were invited. Mrs. Mouse hoped that everything might be pleasant. The mice at the house were rather inclined to hold themselves a little above the field mice, why she could not tell, for she was quite sure one family was as good as the other, and she had no wish to slight either.

Mrs. Mouse felt all of a flutter when the night of the party arrived. She had allowed her four little daughters to stay up for a while and see part of the fun, if they would promise to be good. Very nice and proper they looked standing side by side with their little arms folded. The first to arrive was the mouse who lived in the parlor cup-board. She was very grand indeed in her high-topped bonnet. Grandmother Skipper and her youngest grandchild came next, and after them came Lady Newly-Wed and her husband. On they came, one after the other, until quite a large, merry crowd had gathered in the back yard. The young mice wanted to dance, so partners were chosen, and the merry whirlers went spinning round and around until they were almost ready to drop.

Billy Nibble and Patty Pry grew tired of the dancing and seated themselves on top of the gate. Tucker Gray saw them and he felt jealous, for he had a great fondness for little Patty and did all in his power to coax her from Billy, but she would not come. Then Tucker went off and devoted himself to Polly Pruin. Polly was charmed, for she had been sitting all alone waving her new turkey feather fan. But all at once the fun was brought to a close, the house door was thrown open and out stole old Tom, the big, black cat. Such a scampering you never saw, and no one stopped until he had safely reached his home. It was a shame that they should be so

rudely disturbed in the midst of their fun, for they were having a very gay time all by themselves, and they are such cute and cunning little things that we like to see them enjoy themselves.

The Interrupted Party.

It was little Dot Mouse's birthday. It had been a long while coming, Dot thought, but she was such a young mouse that time to her did not seem to

have wings as maybe she might have imagined it did, had she been a little older.

At any rate, her birthday had come at last, and Dot was a happy little mouse. Now if this birthday was going to be just like any other day in the

week perhaps Dot would not have been so anxious
for it to come, but this was to be a very different
day—great things were to happen.   Mother
Mouse had promised Dot a party.   Dot had never
had a party, although she had been to the Christmas party given by the squirrel, and she remembered that night as the very happiest time in all

her life. Dot would have liked to ask all the
people she knew, but Mother Mouse had very
different views on the subject, and only the mice
that lived next door, and those that lived in the
baker shop across the way had been invited. They
were very glad to come, and the mice from the
baker's shop had promised to bring some dainties
if there was a chance of their carrying them across

without being seen. Yesterday Dot had found
such a pretty frock when she was hunting around

the nursery closet. She often visited that closet,
for nurse sometimes left the lid off the cracker

jar, and Dot was as fond of crackers as the baby.
But this time she forgot all about the crackers, she
was so pleased over the pretty pink gown.   It
must have belonged to a very tiny doll, for it was
just the right size for Dot, and she was such a
little mouse.   When the birthday came Dot rigged
herself in her new dress and sat down to wait for
her guests.   Mother Mouse was so slow fixing her
ruffled cap that Dot felt sure she would not be
ready in time, but Mother Mouse knew there was
no hurry.   By and bye the mice came creeping in
and greeted their little hostess, with best wishes
for a happy birthday.   The mice from the baker's
had been as good as their word, and each had
brought some sweet meat to add to the repast.   So
there was no lack of good things for the feast.
But alas, alas, their fun was soon to be spoiled.
Mother Mouse had just nibbled a hole in the sugar
bag when a squeak from her daughter made her
look up, and there, almost upon them, stood old Tab,
and close behind her on the stairs were her four
little kittens, each one anxious to secure a mouse
for supper.   Then such a hurrying and scurrying
you never saw in all your life.   It was too bad,
for poor little Dot expected such fun at her party.

Lady Nibble's Ball.

SCRATCH! Scratch! Scratch! went the pen of Lady Nibble. It was a quill that had fallen out of the old gander's tail, and the bottle of blueing that the farmer's wife had left on the hanging shelf served splendidly for ink.

Lady Nibble was writing invitations for a ball. The farmer's family were going to give a dance in the new barn. Her Ladyship knew this was so, for she had overheard the folks talking about it when she went into the kitchen cupboard after some cheese. She made up her mind at once that this was the time to entertain her friends, as there would be lots left to eat after the farmer's dance was over. She went right to work and sent invitations far and near.

Dicky Scratch had been invited to play the music. He had a fiddle that had once adorned the children's Christmas tree, but had been thrown out as rubbish, until Dicky found it. Peter Squeak was to call out the figures, his voice was so high and shrill. The old clothes hamper that had been banished from the house would serve as a splendid stand for Dicky and for Peter Squeak also.

Lady Nibble was all in a flutter of excitement

when the night arrived, and how pleased she was when she found so many had responded to her invitation. They came in dress coats, sacque coats, cutaways and some less fortunate came without

coats—but what they wore made no difference, for everything was lovely, and the best of all Old Ratty Scamper and little Mousey Shy danced together perched upon an old dish-pan that had been turned up-side-down. How they all laughed when poor old Ratty forgot the smallness of the space on which he was dancing, and danced entirely off.

They danced by twos and they danced by rights,

and before they could realize it the farmer's guests were going home and Lady Nibble had invited them to step into the barn and partake of refreshments. What a feast they had! Her Ladyship had chosen wisely in selecting this night, for such rich dainties rarely fall to a mouse's lot with so little trouble. There were dainty bits of cheese, crackers, fine chicken and many other nice things, but the very best of all was the box of chocolates which old Ratty Scamper found hidden under the table. He had tasted nothing so good since the Christmas before, when he had crept into little Flossie Gray's bed-room and taken a big bite of the candy cane old St. Nicholas had left in her stocking. Then they found a dish of strawberry ice cream, which someone had left. They had never tasted ice cream before, and at first they were afraid to touch it, but when they once got a taste, they all voted it very nice.

It was all over at last, for even the best of things must end, and as Lady Nibble bade her guests good-night she felt satisfied that this had been the great success of her life.

The Adventure of the Mice.

THINGS had reached a point where something must be done, so thought and so said the four gray mice that had met together to talk over their woes. These four mice had spent their lives in perfect comfort and happiness under the high back steps, and they knew that no four mice were quite as happy as they. But what a change had come into their lives! The house had been sold, and these new people made the lives of these four

little mice most miserable. No such thing as a trap had ever bothered them—but now it was almost impossible to enter a cupboard or to climb up on a shelf without one of these cruel traps coming

PALMER COX

(234)

to view. Of course the cheese smelt good and looked so tempting, but these sly little chaps had learned the danger of traps, and though they wished and sighed for the good things, they did not venture near these strong wire enemies. But worse than traps came into their lives. These they could keep away from, but a foe, big and powerful, had been brought to capture them. It was a large, sharp-eyed, shiney black cat. He never seemed to sleep, for try when they might to creep silently into the house his quick ears heard them, and his big round eyes looked eagerly around. These four little mice were growing as thin as shadows, for they dared not venture from their step home to get even a morsel of food. At last they met in council, and then it was decided that something must be done. After much talking they concluded that puss must be killed and that they must do it. So armed with weapons and a good strong rope they started on their mission. You can't guess how brave they felt nor how sure of their success. But what a difference came when they started into the house. There stood the cat. Then they forgot to be brave and off they scampered, as fast as possible, never stopping to look behind.

Grandmother Mouse's Tale.

GRANDMOTHER MOUSE had invited her two oldest grand-daughters to tea. They were very nice little mice and great favorites with the old lady, and as they also were very fond of their grandmother, it was a pleasure for them to go. They put on their very best clothes and took lots of care in getting ready, for their grandmother was most particular. When they reached the house there she stood on the top one of the back kitchen steps, wearing her ruffled cap and her snowy white apron, and ready with a hearty welcome for both of them.

Grandmother Mouse lived all by herself in the cupboard under the kitchen stairs. This had been her home all her life, and as they sat around the tea table that evening she told them the story of how this became her home.

"Mother," said she, "went off one day to hunt for a bit of cheese or some nice fresh crackers and told me to stay where I was until she came back. I shut my eyes thinking I would take a nap while she was gone, for the time always seemed so dreary when mother was away—and I must have taken a good long nap, for it was dark when I opened my eyes, but mother was not there, though I called and called her.   All that night she did not come,

and when the next day passed and again she did

not come, I knew something had happened to her —but whether the old cat had pounced upon her or whether she yielded to temptation in the form of a piece of cheese and so ended her life in a wicked trap, I never found out." Here Grandmother stopped to wipe her eyes, for though it was a long time ago, she could not tell the story without weeping.

"Well," continued she, "I had grown very hungry by this time, so I stole quietly out to find something to eat. How strange I felt all alone in this new world. I seemed to be growing tinier every minute or else the great big cellar was growing bigger. Cook had made some lovely rusks and had put them in the cellar to cool. This was very kind in cook, I thought, and I ate all the sugar off the top of one and then began to nibble at the crust. But just then I heard footsteps, and oh my! how fast I scampered away. It was cook after the rusks, and I heard her mutter as she went up the stairs, "Mistress must certainly get a trap; the mice have been at work again." I trembled so that I was afraid cook would hear me, and the vision of that trap made me so unhappy that I could not sleep one wink. Then and there I made up my mind that nothing, nothing would ever tempt me to go near a trap, not

the richest piece of cheese, not the daintiest morsel
of cake.   I thought of the cake and cheese, my
dears," said the mouse, smiling, "because they
were the two things I particularly loved, and I
must own that I have not lost my fondness for
them, if I am old and a grandmother.

"Day after day went by, and I was getting
thin, for the vision of the trap had not left my
mind, and I was afraid to venture out for food.
But time is a great healer, you know, so at last I
became quite brave and visited the pantry shelf
nightly.

"By and by I married your grandfather.   His
home was in one corner of the garret back of the
camphor chest.   I spent two nights there, but I
was so homesick that your grandfather said he did
not mind where he lived, and the cupboard under
the stairs was quite good enough for him.   So the
next day back we came, and a happier mouse than
I never lived.

"Your mother was born here and your grandfather died here.   The world is very hard upon
mice, my children, and is forever laying snares for
them to fall into, and in an unlucky moment your
grandfather ate of a piece of meat on which poison
had been spread.   He only lived a little while,
and once more I was left alone, for your mother

married and had gone to live in the next door kitchen. So now," finished grandmother, "you see this has always been my home, and I hope it always will be. But I think it is getting late now and that you had better be going—but come soon again, for you know I am always glad to see you.

The Candle Feast.

THERE was once a little gray mouse who was no larger or older than the other mice, but who was always so bright and clever and so full of all sorts of plans and schemes that the other mice had gotten into the habit of going to her in all their troubles, and she was always ready and pleased to put her little wits to work and to help them the very best she knew how.

And she was such a brave little mouse, too. No matter how bold or how daring the scheme she might suggest, she was always ready to do her part in the undertaking. Now Miss Mousy had been prowling around in the kitchen one morning and had seen the cook busily at work making pies and tarts, and, last of all, brown, spicy ginger snaps. If there was one thing in this world that Miss Mousey dearly loved it was ginger snaps.

It quite made her mouth water to even think about
them, and she made up her mind that when the
house was hushed for the night, and all had gone
to bed, she and her jolly young friends would visit
the kitchen shelf. Well, Miss Mousey knew the
big yellow bowl in which the snaps were kept.

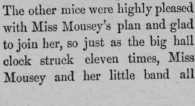

The other mice were highly pleased
with Miss Mousey's plan and glad
to join her, so just as the big hall
clock struck eleven times, Miss
Mousey and her little band all

carefully masked entered the kitchen quietly and
carefully. But the bitterest disappointment awaited
them; high on the shelf stood the ginger snaps,
but not in the yellow bowl. A strong tin box now
held them and the lid was shut down tight. There
they all stood, a sad and disappointed group, their
prize so near and yet beyond their reach. But

16

Miss Mousey was not going to spend her time in fretting, her little bright eyes glanced sharply

around the kitchen to find something else to satisfy the hunger of herself and her sorrowful-looking

friends.   She had almost given up in despair, when
the glow from the fire fell on the table, and there
stood a tall white candle.   It was only the work
of a minute to call the others, and then all fell to
planning a way to carry off their prize.   Finally,
after much pulling and tugging, the candle was
taken from the holder, and then all went to work
with a will to mount it on their shoulders and
bear it away to some undisturbed corner.   It was
a funny sight to see them travelling along with
their queer burden, but they did not mind, and
were only anxious to get back to their home before
they were discovered.   At last they reached the
cellar safe and sound, and then the fun began.
There they stood, one against the other on either
side of the candle, and nibbled away until not a
thing but the string remained.   At first they did
not like the taste of candle very much, but when
they had finished, they one and all decided that it
was not the worst fare in the world after all, and
some of them concluded that they really liked the
candle much better than they did the ginger snaps.
At any rate, they felt repaid for their trouble and
decided that some night they would all go again
to the kitchen and get another candle.

The Mouse's Easter Egg.

IT was spring, and it was Easter time. The mice knew it was Easter because one of them while rummaging in the kitchen cupboard for a nibble

of something had overheard the cook giving the order to the grocer's boy. Miss Mousey had heard her say—"I want a great many eggs, for I have promised to dye some for the children, and besides

Easter is not Easter without plenty of eggs."
The grocer's boy seemed to be of the same opinion,
and cook laughed merrily when he told her how
many he could eat.

Now Miss Mousey made up her mind that if
cook and the grocer's boy found eggs such fine
food, she must certainly try to have one for her
breakfast on Easter day.

Such a commotion as reigned in the kitchen on
Saturday morning! Of course the children had
no school, and they all wanted to help cook. You
should have heard the bursts of gleeful laughter
as the blue and crimson, green, purple and yellow
eggs were put on a platter to cool. Miss Mousey
saw and heard it all as she sat peeping through a
crack in the cupboard door that morning. "If
they will only leave them on the platter until to-
morrow," thought Miss Mousey, "I can easily
help myself, and I know the children will not
mind letting me have just one." Fortune was
good to this little gray lady, and when cook fixed
the fire for the night and turned out the gas, the
eggs still stood on the plate. Now Miss Mousey
knew that her two young brothers would like to
try the eggs just as well as she, so she asked them
to come with her, and armed with knife, fork and
spoon they started on their journey.

It was easy enough to reach the egg, but not quite so easy to take it home. It was so round and so smooth that, try as they might, not one could manage it. At last Miss Mousey jumped for joy—she had hit on a splendid plan. It was

the easiest thing in the world to manage. She would lie down flat on her back, hold the egg with her four little feet, and then her two strong brothers could pull her along by her tail. To think was to act this time and before many minutes the egg was

landed in a safe hiding-place to stay until morning.
Then what a feast they had and how proud the
brothers were to think that all had been so well
managed by their gray sister.

The Monkeys' Trick.

JOCKO AND JERRY were two lively, long-tailed
monkeys that lived with their father and mother
in the sunny, Southern lands. They were the
most mischievous little fellows you could well imagine, and their poor mother punished and scolded
them all the time, but all in vain; hardly a day
passed that Jocko or Jerry did not get into some
kind of trouble.

It was great fun to watch them skipping from
tree to tree in search of the large, yellow bananas
that grew in great quantities near their home, or
climbing after the cocoanuts they so dearly loved,
and which furnished many a dainty meal for the
hungry youngsters.

Jocko and Jerry seemed never to be still. If
they were not jumping from limb to limb of the
tall forest trees they were swinging from the
branches by their tails, which they twisted securely
around the limbs, or else they were cutting up

some other kind of caper.   When night came they
needed no rocking, for so tired were they that they

hardly had time to settle themselves for the night
before they were in dreamland.

Brown Bruin was a solemn, dignified bear that dwelt in the forest where the monkey family lived. He had grown so fat in his old age that his greatest pleasure was to take things easy. Hurrying and scurrying were not to his liking, and the merry, chattering ways of Jocko and Jerry bothered him no little. He had many times talked to them, and tried to show them how much better it was to live a quiet, peaceful life. The little monkeys listened to all he said, and they seemed so solemn that Brown Bruin felt sure his words had not been in vain; but time showed him his mistake.

Old Bruin had among his possessions a beautiful red hammock that he prized very highly, not only for itself, but for the many happy hours he had spent in it. He swung it up one morning as usual, and, placing his high hat on the ground beneath, crawled into the hammock to read his morning paper and take a little nap. Jocko and Jerry watched the bear preparing to spend a comfortable morning and decided to play a trick on him. So they sat very quietly, hidden among the leaves, until Bruin was lost in the reading of his paper. Poor fellow! he was so deeply engaged in reading the report of the stock market and wondering whether he would not be able to indulge in a little veal, mutton and pork, now they were going so low, that he had not noticed that the monkeys were

near.   They stole down, and Jocko with his sharp

little knife cut the rope, and down went Mr. Bruin all in a heap. How these merry little monkeys did chatter and laugh when they saw the old fellow on the ground, but they had good sense enough to run away as fast as they could go, for they knew, if they were caught, they would get a good scolding, and they should have a good hard scolding, for they were very naughty monkeys, indeed, to disturb the poor bear in his hammock.

Poor Bruin did not know what to make of it when he found himself suddenly landed on his head on the hard ground, but he soon made up his mind that it was all a trick which mischievous Jocko and Jerry had played on him, and he felt very badly to think that his fine silk hat was ruined and his hammock injured just through the work of frolicsome monkeys, and he decided that he would find some other place to spend his leisure, where he would not be troubled by such naughty little creatures as Jocko and Jerry.

The Magpie's Revenge.

It was all due to the treatment which Madame Magpie had received at the time of the great ball in the early spring. Invitations had been sent

far and near, and she had been slighted. Why,
she could not guess—not because she had been forgotten, she was sure of that, for had she not whispered to all the birds in the forest that she was
most anxious to attend this wonderful dance. The
Ostrich was one of the committee, and she knew
she had told him of her wish. At last the truth
slipped out—one and all thought she talked too
much. Madame Magpie felt very badly about it,
but she decided to keep perfectly quiet, make no
fuss, and see if a time would not come when she
might punish these folks who called themselves
her friends. The days of spring passed by, and
one by one the summer months came creeping on,
and still Madame Magpie could think of no plan
that just exactly pleased her. At last she hit upon
something that suited her perfectly.

Her first movement was to provide herself with
writing material. She needed no pen, for her own
wing served that purpose. Then she proceeded to
write a host of invitations. It kept her busy for
several days, but at last all was finished and each
sent to the proper person.

You see, Madame Magpie had decided to give
a feast, and she had also decided to let these folks
who thought she talked too much see how much
she really could talk.

At last the day and hour arrived, and the guests came in crowds. The little hostess had spared no pains in securing all sorts of good things, and when all were come, and had taken their places, and were ready to enjoy the feast, the Madame's fun began. She commenced chattering at such a

lively rate that the guests were almost distracted. She rattled on and on, and on, her voice growing louder and shriller every minute, until one by one the animals rushed away almost deafened by the Magpie s shrieks. Not one was brave enough to stay, and although the Magpie's throat was raw, she felt she was revenged.

The Search for Food.

"Tick Tock! Tick tock! Tick tock!" slowly and steadily the hands of the kitchen clock moved for-

ward, but still it kept on with its oft-repeating song. Madame Mouse felt as though she could stand

it no longer. About two hours ago her husband
had crept cautiously out of the cupboard and
across the kitchen floor, and had stolen quietly
down cellar, hoping to find lots to eat for his wife
and hungry little ones. Madame Mouse was growing very nervous. The cellar was not so far away
that he must be gone two hours. She longed to
go to the cellar herself and see what could have
become of him, but she dared not leave her little
ones alone. Just as the clock struck again

Madame Mouse, who was taking another peep,
spied her husband moving slowly across the room,
the empty bag at his side. He had gone to the
cellar but had not found a single thing. He
guessed then that the folks had gone away on a
visit, and had left nothing behind them, not even
the tiniest morsel to reward his search. Madame
Mouse and her husband put their heads together
to try to think of some plan for finding food for
their hungry babies. At last they decided that
Father Mouse should try the big hall closet. He

had once found there a lunch basket belonging to one of the children, and there was quite a lot in it, too. As soon as he went into the closet a half dozen heads or more peeped out from holes in the floor. "You've come to a sorry place for food," said they, "we are almost starved."

Mr. Mouse said not a word but turned towards home. Having heard from her husband that the folks were away, Mrs. Mouse and her four babies had ventured out. Mr. Mouse saw them as soon as he entered the kitchen. Tiny was in his mother's arms, while Tip, Top and Teddy huddled around her. "Iam too big a coward," thought Mr. Mouse, "to go back to them empty handed," so he stole away without their having seen him.

He wandered about the shed, wondering what next to do, when all at once his eyes spied something round and white gleaming at him from the corner. "Luck at last," thought he, and it was, too, for it proved to be a long white candle. A few seconds brought him to his family, the good news was told, and they all hurried away to have a royal feast. It seemed such a treat after the long waiting and the tedious search they had had, and they all felt very thankful, even baby Tiny who sat in his mother's arms and quietly nibbled away at his share,

was beginning to feel pretty heavy. Fred wanted
to help him, but Tom insisted on carrying it all
alone, too proud to own that he was tired. At
length the cottage where Jerry lived came in sight,
and before long they lifted the latch of the gate
and walked up the gravel walk to the house.
How pleased Jerry was to see them, and how full
of delight over the basket of goodies! Jerry had

a funny new pet to show the boys that day—a wee
little pig that he had taught to come into the
kitchen and drink milk from a saucer.

The boys had a fine time, and when they said
good-bye to Jerry they promised him and themselves, too, that it would not be long before they
came again.

The opportunity to again pay a visit to Jerry
came in the course of a few months, and bright
and early one Saturday the boys started on their

trip. Jerry was delighted to see them, but they
found him in so much trouble that they really
pitied him. It was all on account of the pig that
had been so cute and pretty when they visited him
before. He had sent them a photograph of piggy
as he looked when performing his tricks, and they
fully expected to see him dance and play the fiddle.
This was one great reason they were so anxious to
go out to Jerry's once more, for they were wild to
see this wonderful creature about whom they had
heard so much.

As they drew near the house, they heard the pig
squealing and grunting at a great rate, while above
all the din rose the voice of Jerry, evidently in no
very pleasant frame of mind. Opening the door,
they beheld Jerry standing, hat in hand, and looking very much troubled. Tables and chairs were
overturned, and the stove-pipe was just falling
down, while the stove lay upset on the floor. In
the midst of it all stood a great ugly hog, so huge
that it seemed to fill the whole room. The boys
were thunderstruck to see such a big hog in the
house and wondered how it got there. Then Jerry
explained to them that this was the little pig of
which they had all been so fond. It had kept
growing and growing, and every day he had
thought he would put it out of doors, but he had

not done it, and now it was more of a task than he could do alone. The boys offered to help him, and together they drove the pig to the door, but

alas, alas, he was so big that all he could get outside the cottage door was his head. He would have been very glad to get out, for the house was uncomfortably small, but try as he might, he could get no further. So they decided to set to work and take down a portion of the wall so as to make a place large enough for him to get out. It was a good deal of work, and by the time they got the work all done it was growing dark and time for the boys to be starting for home. They felt that they had had a very exciting day, take it all in all, and they were glad that they happened to be on hand to help Jerry in his time of trouble, and Jerry was no less pleased to think that he had had such good helpers.

Out in the Storm.

LITTLE LETTY LEE had come to Aunt Ruth's

to spend her vacation. Aunt Ruth and Uncle William lived on a great big farm, and they gladly

(263)

welcomed their little niece, for they loved her dearly. It made them very happy to hear her merry voice and to watch her as she ran joyfully around the place. She made friends with the cows, patted the horses as they stood in their stables, and she even made visits to the pen where the old mother pig and her ten little ones dwelt.

But Letty loved the chickens best of all. She never tired of watching them, and she would hop out of bed at the first call to help Aunt Ruth scatter the corn for the breakfast of this hungry flock. She would jump with delight when Aunt Ruth called, "Chick! Chick! Chick!" and hens and roosters, and chickens of all sizes, came running from every direction. Another of Letty's amusements was to hunt for the eggs. What funny places the hens choose sometimes! Letty felt sure they were trying to hide from her. One day she came to the house with fourteen new-laid eggs in her basket. "Now," said Aunt Ruth, "let's go right away and put these under old Biddy, and the first chick she hatches out shall be yours." Letty watched every day, and by and by the shell was broken and out came a tiny baby bird. Letty was so pleased. One morning a heavy shower fell and Letty's little chick got lost from the rest. Uncle William found him when

(265)

he came in from the barn. The poor baby was
sitting on a fence post almost drowned. Letty
wrapped him in soft flannel, tucked him away in
a basket, and in an hour or so he was jumping
around as lively as ever. Oh, how delighted she
was, for she feared the poor little fellow would die.

In the Meadow.

BESIDE the brook that flowed through the
meadow, bubbling and rippling along day after
day, grew a young tree. It had suffered greatly
during the long, cold winter, and it sometimes
grew so tired of Jack Frost's pinches and his
strong, icy breath that it wanted to die. But now
old Jack Frost had left the meadow and gone far
north to his snow-clad home, and the warm, gentle
sun smiled so sweetly upon the little tree that it
felt like growing and blooming again, and one by
one it put forth its little leaves until it was fully
decked in its soft, green gown.

A robin saw the pretty tree one day, and thought
what a fine home he and his bride might find
among its branches. So he went busily to work
and soon the dearest little nest rested snugly
almost in the top of the tree, and when it was fin-

ished he brought home his mate, and the tree was very proud to think that it had been selected as the home of such a loving pair. But one day

something happened that made the little birds happy, too, and this is what it was: For some time four tiny blue eggs had been carefully tended by the robins, and at last four little beaks picked the shell and four little baby robins came out to live in this great, big world. The tree rocked them gently, and the mother thought that no baby robins ever had a prettier cradle than hers. The robin family stayed in the tree all summer, and the tree kept growing stronger and stronger, and taller and taller, and when the birdies flew away it was only comforted by the promise that the old birds would come back again the next year. Just before he flew away the old robin lingered beneath the tree just long enough to sing a farewell song.

Down by the very brook over which hung the tree, which was the home of the robins, dwelt a handsome green frog. He was born there in the early spring, and before the robins came the tree had watched little Froggy-woggy with great interest. It wondered to see him growing so fast, and he looked so jolly with his great grinning mouth and his big, bulging eyes. Just as soon as the sun reached the banks of the little brook Froggy would perch himself on a smooth stone, blinking and winking as though the world gave nothing but happiness to him. Now the tree soon learned that Froggy loved a little lady frog. Every morning went the youthful lover to take his lady love for a walk; he carried a huge bou-

quet of flowers so beautiful that the bees and butterflies followed him, sipping of their sweetness.
One day Froggy and his lady love went away and
never came back again. The tree felt sure they
had found a home for themselves by some other
stream.

A hill sloped up from the brookside, and among

the grasses and low shrubs flowers of all sorts
lifted their heads. Daisies opened their bright
eyes at the peep of morning, and nodded their
sleepy little heads at the coming of the shadows.
The blue violets shyly put forth their bloom, and
the yellow buttercups sparkled and gleamed in the
bright sunshine. But the hillside was most beauti-

ful when the children coming home from school stopped to gather the posies. Their chatter and joyous laughter rang out like the sweetest music, as beautiful, so thought the tree, as the song of the birds that sang so sweetly all day long.

One night the flowers and trees were awakened from their happy dreams by the strangest noise they had ever heard. The moon was big and round that night and was shedding her brightest light, so that the meadow was almost as bright as day. Flowers lifted their drowsy heads, and the trees bent and swayed to peep around each other to find out, if possible, the cause of so much trouble. They soon discovered that a flock of young birds that had doubtless wandered from their nests and had stayed out too late had been attacked by some big, round-eyed owls, and the loud cry of fear from the young birds as they hurried through the air had wakened all the sleeping hillside and put sleep to flight.

But the meadow was not only the home of the birds, the flowers and the fat little frogs, but the children used to go there and spend the long beautiful summer days playing in the soft, green grass hunting for the birds' nests and gathering the bright, pretty flowers. But, best of all, they loved to chase the butterflies that flitted here and there,

drinking the honey from the flower cups, and resting lightly on the nodding grasses. Take it all in
all, the meadow was the most delightful place in
the world, not only for the children, but for all the
merry crowds of birds and insects that made it their
home and their pleasure ground, and none of them
would have known how to get along without it.

The Lost Prize.

KITTY GRAY had been brought to her new

home in a covered basket. She remembered well
how one of the boys had brought a saucer of new

milk to the barn, set it down on the floor, and, when she and her brothers and sisters were busy

lapping up the milk, she had been picked up, carried to the house, and tucked away in the basket.

It was hours before she was taken out. Time

and time again had she called "Mew! Mew!" just as loud as ever she could, but it had done no

good, a gentle voice would always say, "Lie still,
Kitty Gray, and be real good."

When the basket was opened and Kitty jumped
out she found herself in a place very different
from the big barn in which she had always lived.
But she soon grew to like it very much. She

loved the warm fire, beside which she curled herself every night, and the cook gave her lots of
good things to eat.

Cook sat by the fire reading one night, and
Kitty lay curled up in her lap. Kit's eyes roamed
lazily around the room until they rested upon an
empty pickle bottle that cook had left standing on

the dresser. What was that black object that kept moving around in the bottle? "As sure as you are living," thought Kitty Gray, "that is a mouse. I'll wait until cook goes to bed, and then I'll have a feast."

The clock struck ten, and cook put out the light and went up stairs. Kit jumped up on the dresser, peeped in at the mouse, stuck her paw in the bottle, but no mouse came out. Then Kitty shook the bottle, then she turned it upside down, but the mouse would not shake out. Then Kit grew cross, and seizing the bottle, brought it down crash on a flat iron that lay near. It flew in a hundred pieces, and away scampered the mouse, right through a hole in the wall, and so swiftly that Kitty had no chance at it at all. She was dread-

fully disappointed, but that did not help matters, so she curled herself in a heap by the fire to forget her troubles in sleep, but in the future she will have too much good sense to strike a bottle on an iron.

Rival Babies.

DADDY BEAR had gone off on a hunting trip.
He had left Madam Bear and their little son alone,
but he had brought such a fine young lamb from
the neighboring farm-yard that he had no fear of
their being in want while he was gone.

Daddy Bear and his wife were very proud of
their young son. They thought nothing so beautiful as his fat little body and his sharp little eyes,
that looked so bright and charming. His funny
attempts to growl like his parents made them both
laugh merrily.

Very near to the home of the bears dwelt another family. This family consisted of Father
and Mother Fox and their little son. Now the
Fox parents were just as fond and proud of their
baby as Daddy and Madam Bear were of theirs,
and they used often to think that their son was
just a little more cute than Baby Bear. These
two little chaps were born about the same time,
and each had been carefully watched and guarded
by its fond parents, who tried to outdo each other
in their devotion to their babies. If Madam Bear
took her little boy walking, young Master Fox
was soon taken out for a stroll. If little Foxy
appeared in a new Pinafore, Madam Bear lost no

time in arraying her son in one just like it.   So it
went on, and these rival babies grew strong and
hearty, caring not at all for the jealousies of their
mothers, but spending many happy hours together
in play.

One day the two mothers and the two babies
met together in the woods.   The youngsters played
happily together, while the mothers sat on a fallen
log and chatted.   Finally Mother Bear declared
that her son was the taller.   Mother Fox said that
could not be the case, for she knew that honor belonged to Foxy.   So the little folks were called
and made to stand up and be measured, but it did
no good, for each mother claimed that her son was
the taller.   At last they decided to leave the matter to some friends that happened to be passing,
and they decided that there was no difference between them.   This did not satisfy the mothers, and
each one thought that the honor belonged to them.

The Dance in the Woods.

IT was spring, and the butterflies now began to
emerge from the warm, soft covering in which
they had been folded.   They were the pictures of
graceful beauty as they flitted here and there from

flower to flower. The flowers nodded to them
and gave them their sweetest juices to drink. The
birds watched them one morning as they danced
merrily on the green grass, still sparkling with the
early dew.

"It seems to me," said a young raven, "that

if the butterfly can whirl so gracefully on his tiny
legs, we also might learn to perform this most delightful accomplishment."

The raven prided himself upon his shiny black
coat, and it is likely he thought this a good chance
of showing off before his friends.

"Let's try it once," said the stork, who was out

for a stroll and had stopped to watch the merry
butterflies.

"We will dance together," said the raven. So
the stork threw his long bill over the raven's
shoulder, and wing to wing they whirled around,
not pictures of grace, however, for they moved
very, very awkwardly.

The eagle, gazing from his lofty nest, saw the
antics of the pair and laughed merrily to himself.
"I'll fly down and get nearer the fun," said he.
Down he came, and meeting a plump, white goose,
he told him of the performance and asked him to
come along and see it. The goose had hard work
to keep up with the eagle, who walked along with

great rapid strides.   The dancers soon grew tired,
but not discouraged, and so, after resting their
weary legs and gaining once more their breath,
they went at it again.

By this time quite a crowd of birds of one sort

or another had perched themselves on trees and
bushes, for such a sight as two birds dancing together was new and strange in the woods of Fly-
away.

A little blue jay, who sat swinging on a bough
of a young cherry tree, thought if it were such

fun to watch the stork and the raven, how much more fun it would be to trip it with them. So down he flew and commenced spinning around and around. This movement on the part of the jay put the hawk in the notion, and she also joined the dancers. The dodo and the crane were the next to fall in, and before very long couple after couple were hopping around enjoying the lively reel.

The Surprise Party.

DEAR me, did no one tell you about the party? It was a perfect success all through. That funny little turtle that lives in the swamp back of the hedgehog's got it up. One morning he arose bright and early, did his work as quickly as possible, and then started around to his friend's, the porcupine, to make him a visit. "Do you know," said the turtle, after a while, "I've been thinking how pleasant it would be to get up a surprise party for our neighbor, Mr. Bruin."

"The very thing," replied the porcupine, "if you are willing to invite the people."

"I'll be glad to do it," answered the turtle. The turtle would not stay to dinner, although the porcupine invited him, and that very afternoon he

started off to invite the guests. The following
Monday was selected, and everybody was charged
not to let the news reach the ears of Mrs. Bruin.

Monday came bright and clear, and about eight
o'clock all the guests met at the weeping willow
tree and started off together. They looked very

funny as they marched along, each one carrying
his basket on his arm.   These baskets were carefully guarded, for therein were hidden all sorts of
dainties for the feast to be given during the evening.   When they reached the house, Jedekiah Fox
knocked at the door, and instead of opening it Mr.

Bruin popped his head out of the window.   You
never saw anybody so surprised in your life.   But
what lots of fun they did have after they had gone
in and put down their baskets!   The bear was so
glad to see them that he consented to show them
how he used to dance when he travelled around
with Prof. Trix.   So he took his cane in his hand

and performed many queer antics, which were exceedingly amusing to the whole company. They were all so happy and time passed so pleasantly that the wee, small hours of the morning dawned before the party broke up. They all agreed that the turtle deserved much praise for the fine time he had been the means of affording them, and decided to arrange a surprise party for him some day.

The Raid of the Rats.

THERE was once a man named Nathan Brown, who kept the "Silver Lake Mill." The mill had been so named on account of the beautiful stream of water upon whose banks it was built. This water as it flowed on and on, day after day, turned the great wheel and ground the wheat that the farmers brought to Nathan to be made into flour. Nathan was a big, fat, red-cheeked fellow, who loved nothing better than a chat with his neighbors, and while the mill wheel kept busily and steadily turning the dusty miller kept up a merry chattering.

One day Nathan looked very solemn, and the farmer who had come with his bag of wheat wondered what had happened. He asked no ques-

tions, for he knew that in time the miller would
tell him.   When Nathan had emptied the wheat
into the hopper he sat down beside the farmer and
began to talk.   "Do you know," said he, "there
is something carrying off my wheat, and what it
is I don't know, but I have my suspicions that it
is the rats.   I have about made up my mind to
set traps and see if I can in that way discover who
the thieves may be."

Now it happened that the rats were the doers
of all the mischief, and it also happened that one
of them, who had taken a nap on a beam, wakened
in time to hear what the miller said.

"Traps?" thought he, "that ends the fun for
us.   We will carry off all we can to-night, and
then get away from this place."   Just as soon as
old Ratty could leave without being seen he hurried off to tell the rest of the rats the news he had
heard.   They all agreed that they must get away

as soon as possible, but, like him, they wanted one
more night of fun.

When night came a big crowd had gathered.
They had merry times chasing one another, in and
out among the bags, and crawling up them and
sliding down again.

"I have an idea," said one of the rats; "I think

if we tried we might manage to carry away one of
those small bags of flour. We could hide it in
the wagon house and have a merry time with it."

"That's a splendid idea," cried they all; "we
can do it if we try."

One of the smallest bags was selected, and all
went to work, and they did work. It was not
easy to lift the sack up on their shoulders, nor to

keep it there.   One failure followed another, but these little fellows would not give up, and they tried and tried again, until at last success rewarded their efforts, and they started to the wagon house.

Now the shortest road to the wagon house was by way of the ledge outside of the large mill door. They crept along, carefully balancing the sack, when all at once the bag slipped, and over all of them went down into the stream below.   The flour was forgotten, and each one's mightiest effort was devoted to saving himself.   They had a good hard pull, but at last all stood shivering and shaking on the bank, the sorriest looking crowd of rats you ever saw.   They got together a lot of sticks and leaves and built a fire, and soon looked quite themselves again—but the flour was gone, and all agreed that they had paid very dearly for their fun.

The Back Yard Party.

Mrs. Mouse laid down her pen and breathed a sigh of relief. She had been busily at work getting out invitations for a grand garden party in the back yard, and now she had finished. The field mice, the mice at the barn and wagon house, and, of course, the house mice, all were invited.

Mrs. Mouse hoped that everything might be
pleasant. The mice at the house were rather inclined to hold themselves a little above the field
mice, why she could not tell, for she was quite
sure one family was as good as the other, and she
had no wish to slight either.

Mrs. Mouse felt all of a flutter when the night
of the party arrived. She had allowed her four
little daughters to stay up for a while and see
part of the fun if they would promise to be good.
Very nice and proper they looked standing side by
side with their little arms folded. The first to
arrive was the mouse who lived in the parlor cupboard. She was very grand, indeed, in her high-
19

topped bonnet. Grandmother Skipper and her
youngest grandchild came next, and after them
came Lady Newly-Wed and her husband. On
they came, one after the other, until quite a large,
merry crowd had gathered in the back yard. The
young mice wanted to dance, so partners were

chosen, and the merry whirlers went spinning
round and round until they were almost ready to
drop.

Billy Nibble and Patty Pry grew tired of dancing and seated themselves on top of the gate.
Tucker Gray saw them, and he felt jealous, for he

had a great fondness for little Patty and did all in
his power to coax her away from Billy, but she
would not come.   Then Tucker went off and devoted himself to Polly Pruin.   Polly was charmed,

for she had been sitting all alone, waving her new
turkey feather fan.   But all at once the fun was
brought to a close, the house door was thrown
open, and out stole old Tom, the big, black cat.
Such a scapering you never saw, and no one

stopped until he had safely reached his home. It was a shame that they should be so rudely disturbed in the midst of their fun, for they were having a very gay time all by themselves, and they are such cute and cunning little things that we like to see them enjoy themselves.

Bruin's Singing School.

You will really be quite surprised when I tell you how Uncle Bear started the singing school at Matchless Hollow. It happened in this way. One real cold winter night, when the snow lay on the ground like a great white blanket, quite a number of young people made up a sleighing party. It was the first sleighing of the winter, and everybody was extremely anxious to go. What lots of fun they had as they sped over the hard, white crust! After a while some of the folks began holding their ears and rubbing their hands together in a manner that showed they were far from warm. "Wouldn't it be jolly," some one called out, "to stop at Uncle Bear's." "Oh, do," came from all sides. It did not take them long to reach the home of the Bears, but it did take some time to rouse the old folks from the

sound sleep into which they had fallen. Both the
old people seemed glad to see their young friends,
and the warm fire soon sent the blood tingling
through their young bodies. " Won't you give us

a song," said Auntie Bear, " Uncle and I are so
fond of music." It took them some time to get
started, but after a while they began, and they
sung very merrily. One song after another was

sung, and then Uncle Bear asked them why they
did not have a singing school. He was willing to
lead them, he said, for he did not think he had
forgotten all he had learned when he was young.
Everybody was delighted, and an evening was set
for the following week. With many thanks for
the kind reception they had received, the young

people started off, singing a farewell song as they
gathered together out in the moonlight.

They wanted everybody to know about this
singing school they were to have every Tuesday
evening in the Hollow, so on their way home they
arranged to get Bonny Bun, the white rabbit, to
carry invitations to all the dwellers of the forest.
This he could do very easily, for he wore a pair of

snow-shoes which helped him to get over the
ground very quickly. Everybody was invited,
even to the birds, and such a crowd as gathered in
the Hollow was enough to fill Uncle Bear's heart
with delight. He arranged them in a circle and
began to sing, starting out with a familiar song
about the hunter and his gun. After one or two
songs he said they must settle down to business.
He said they had better put all their time for this
one evening on the scale, so he made each one sing
it alone, then altogether, while he stood beating
time with his soft, fat hand. Then he told the
animals to keep quiet and listen to a quintette of
birds that were perched on a nearby tree. These
birds sang a very beautiful song that made the
woods ring with melody.

Indeed, it was so very beautiful that the other
animals were almost afraid to try their voices after-
ward. However, they all did the best they could
to follow the instructions of their leader.

When the hour for closing came they all agreed
that they had spent a very pleasant evening, and
voted to come again the next week. This was the
beginning of a singing school, the like of which
had not been known in many years. The singing
shool proved to be a very popular thing, and before the winter was over there were hundreds of

the young folks of the forest attending it. The
greatest part of the fun was the going and coming,
and this was especially delightful to the young
lovers, and in the spring there were many wed-
dings as a result.

Adventures of the Mice.

NIGHT had come, and the Nibble Family had
all returned to their home in the front cellar. By
and by some of the neighbors dropped in, until
quite a party had gotten together.

"We had a feast,"
said Lady Nibble, "but
no danger attended it.
We found a whole
cheese on the pantry
shelf with not a sign
of a cover over it. It
would have been folly
to miss such a chance
as this, so we went to
work and ate until we
could hardly move. If it is not carried off we
hope to have another feast to-morrow."

"Do you know, I almost lost my life to-day,"

said a very young mouse, "and I'll tell you how;

I saw the most tempt-
ing piece of cheese in
the centre of a funny
red box; so I put my
head in to take a bite,
and, bless you, a spring
snapped down and held
me tight. I jumped
around and around
with this thing on my
head, and shook it as
hard as ever I could,
although I was nearly
choked to death, but I
could not get out. At
last, by some rare good
fortune, the wire that
held the spring broke
and set me free. It
was a narrow escape,
and it taught me a
good lesson. Never,
as long as I live, will I
venture near a trap."

"We had quite a scare, too," spoke up one of
the young Squeaks. "My brothers and I crawled

into the jail to see what we could find to eat. We often pick up crumbs there. Well, this morning we found more than crumbs—we had quite a fine breakfast of cold potatoes, bread and a pitcher of milk. We were so interested in our eating that we did not hear a sound until a shadow made me look up, and I saw a big yellow cat coming towards us. I ran, a piece of bread still in my

mouth, and called to my brothers, and all of us had just time enough to get out of the clutches of that huge yellow monster."

"As you are all relating experiences," said another mouse, "I might as well tell mine. I strolled out in the wheat field to-day, and there on a sheaf of wheat sat a dozen or more of our cousins, the field mice, nibbling away at the grain. They asked me to join them; so I did, and I really had

a very pleasant time. If you have a chance, visit
them some day. You will like them and the
grain also."

"Speaking of something to eat"—this from
Bobby Nibble—"makes me think of the egg
which three of us boys found. We found it in
the school house play ground, and we ate every bit
of it. It had been cooked, I suppose, for some
fellow's lunch. Why he left it I don't know, but,
at any rate, we found it and had a jolly good time
with it."

"I carried off a jam pie this afternoon," said
Tommy Scratch, "and if you will come across to
my house I will share it with you." No one needed
a second invitation nor a bit of coaxing. Away
they all scampered, thinking that the end of the
day was to be the best part. And they enjoyed the
feast to the fullest extent, for it was not often that
they had such a treat as this. They thought Tommy
must have been very brave to dare to carry off a
whole pie. They looked upon him as sort of a
hero, and were very polite to him all through the
evening.

The little mice must have kept very late hours
that night, for all night long could be heard the
sound of their little feet as they scampered here
and there.

Cousin Bear's Party.

MR. AND MRS. BRUIN had received an invitation to a party. One of the Bear Cousins, who lived back of the hill, had invited them, and Mrs. Bruin told her husband that they must not fail to

go, for it would undoubtedly be a grand affair if the Bears gave it. As soon as possible Mr. Bruin ordered a new suit of clothes from his tailor, a hat from his hatter, and a pair of the most stylish

slippers from his shoemaker. These, with his fine
twisted cane, made up a very fine costume. Mrs.
Bruin immediately summoned her dressmaker, and
together they fashioned a gorgeous crimson gown.
Her bonnet of fine white straw was lined with red,
and, to her delight, her fond husband bought her
a fine feathered fan.

The night of the party Mr. Bruin and his loving wife started off in high glee. As they went
along they were the objects of great admiration.
Mrs. Bruin wore two magnificent sun flowers in
her belt. The night was perfect. The moon was
shining brightly, and the snow beneath their feet
sparkled like diamonds. It was quite a long walk,
but the house was finally reached, and a most delightful time they had. Game followed game in
quick succession, until the call to supper sounded
in their ears. The refreshments were superb. Mr.
Bruin declared that he had never eaten such pork,
so tender and juicy, and the lamb was perfect.
Cousin Bear whispered to Mrs. Bruin that she had
gotten the pork from their neighbor, the farmer,
while the lamb had been procured seven miles away.
It was very late when the Bruins started for home,
and as they sauntered along beneath the stars they
agreed that the party was a great success, and
were more than glad to think that they had gone.

Cock Robin.

COCK ROBIN.

Who killed Cock Robin,

Where the lilies grow?

COCK ROBIN.
With Variations and Illustrations

PALMER COX

Cock Robin Lying in State.

I, said the sparrow,
With my bow and arrow,
I laid him low.

Who saw him die
In the cedar top?
I, said the frog,
As I sat on a log,
In company with others,
I saw him drop.

Who was at hand
To catch his blood?
I, said the owl,
With my big bowl,
I caught the flood.

Who'll make a shroud
  So costly and fine?
    I, said the beetle,
      With my thread and needle,
        The task shall be mine.

Who'll dig a grave
  In the yew-tree shade?
    I, said the mole,
      Will soon make a hole,
        I'll dig the grave.
          With my pickax and spade.

Who'll toll the bell
  In the chapel tower?
    I, said the daw,
      With my long claw,
     I toll the bell
       For half an hour.

Who'll bear a blazing
  Torch in the case?
    I, said the kite,
      Will carry the light
      And show the way
       To the burial place.

Who'll bear the pall
　　Both careful and slow?
　　　I, said the stork,
　　　　With a measured stride,
　　　　My legs are long
　　　　　And my shoulders wide,
　　　　　I'll bear the pall
　　　　　　To the plain below.

Who'll sing a psalm
　　As the hearse goes by?
　　　I, said the thrush,
　　　　If others will hush,
　　　　I'll sing a verse
　　　　　Will bring tears
　　　　　To the eye.

Who'll be the parson
  With faith and trust?
    I, said the rook,
      Will read from my book,
        "Ashes to ashes,
          And dust to dust."

Who'll mark
  The songster's earthy bed?
    I, said the bat,
      Will attend to that.
        I'll carve his name
          On the tree at his head.

Who'll keep it green
   When summer is here?
      I, said the hare
         Will plant flowers there,
            I'll keep it green
               Through many a year.

Who suffered for his fault,
   Ere a week rolled by?
      Who, but the sparrow
         That shot the fatal arrow
            And roused the indignation
               Of all creatures
                  Far and nigh.

The Narrow Escape.

MR. AND MRS. GRAYCOAT and the four little Graycoats lived in the garret of a big, roomy, old farm house. There were great chests up there, around which the little mice played tag, and corners dark and dreary in which they often hid. Fine times these four-footed little fellows enjoyed scampering around wherever they pleased in this their garret home.

Mrs. Graycoat was a nice little mouse and very fond of her husband and four little children, as they were also of her. Mr. Graycoat thought his wife very beautiful when she put on the pink calico mob cap that had once been the property of Charlotte, the bisque doll from Paris. Father Mouse's coat was also part of the wardrobe of one of the dolls, and fitted him so tight he could scarcely breathe in it, but still he was very proud of his rig and wore it whenever he went to market. Father Mouse did the marketing, while Mother Mouse stayed at home with the four little Graycoats, for they were such mischievous little chaps it was not wise to leave them alone. The marketing was done in the pantry or else at the great hanging shelf by the cellar stairs. Father Graycoat carried a bag over his arm into which he

dropped one morsel after another for the wife and babies at home.

One morning he started on his daily raid, his bag over his arm, and his tight-fitting coat buttoned snugly around him, promising the little Graycoats to come back soon and to bring a nibble of cake to each of them if they would be very good children.   He had been gone some time when Mrs. Graycoat put on her pink cap and gathered the little ones around her to wait for his coming. Long and long they waited, and the babies were growing as hungry as little bears, and cross, too, for they wanted the promised cake ; but no Father Graycoat came.   What could have happened ? The little mother was getting anxious, for he had never been gone so long before.   By and by came the patter of well-known feet, and there stood Mr. Graycoat, breathless and empty handed and trembling like a leaf.   Such a time as he had had !   A great white cat had taken possession of the cellar and had led old Graycoat a long and weary chase. Hunger was forgotten then, for Mother Graycoat had time to think of nothing but their happiness in having the father home safe and sound.

The Sick Lion.

THE King of the Forest had been sick for weeks, and every day he grew thinner and thinner —so thin that you could count his ribs, and his great jaw-bones stood out sharp and bold from underneath his shaggy mane. He could not eat, and he could not sleep, and he was becoming so cross and surly that his friends and neighbors dared not go near him. He had long ceased to wander through the forest, and his roar, once so strong and mighty, now sounded like a feeble groan.

The beasts all pitied their poor sick king, for though they feared him, they had always thought him a very handsome fellow, and were proud of his bold and daring ways. But now they felt that all was over, and that it would not be long before the poor old lion would lie down to die. Now one bright sunshiny day the Rhinoceros left his home some way down the river to take a good long swim and perhaps call upon his friends who lived on the other side. The swim was a long one, and the sun was growing very warm, so when he reached the spot where his friends lived he was most happy to stop there to rest and refresh himself. The Rhinoceros knew the Lion,

(319)

and after the gentle breezes had fanned him and
he had grown cool and comfortable he went to
visit him. Such a hopeless object as the Rhinoceros found—he scarcely knew him. "He
will surely die," thought the Rhinoceros, "I
must try to do something for him," and he thought
and thought, until at last he hit upon a plan that
pleased him very much. "My friend," said he,
"will you go home with me? I am sure if you
had a change you would soon be yourself again,
and it is much cooler where I live. If you will
only consent you can mount my back and we will
swim down the river in a little while." It was a
long while before the poor old king would yield,
but he did at last, and the Rhinoceros took such
good care of him, and his house was so cool and
pleasant, that the Lion soon got well and strong.